Blaze of Fury

When Jubal Thorne decided to settle down and become a farmer in Oasis Valley, he was not to know the truth. Tired of being a gun-toting hero to some and a villain to others, the former bounty hunter looked forward to a peaceful life on his dead brother's farm. He might have wanted peace, but when a man has a past like that of Jubal Thorne it isn't long before Fate comes knocking on his door. It all starts with a stray bullet that just misses his head, and ends in a Blaze of Fury for those who underestimated the man they were trying to kill. In his search for the killers, and in defence of what is his own, Thorne shows that the bounty hunter might leave his profession but his profession will never leave *him*.

D0513918

Blaze of Fury

Alexander Frew

A Black Horse Western

ROBERT HALE

ISBN 978-0-7198-2128-8

The Crowood Press
The Stable Block
Crowood Lane
Ramsbury
Marlborough
Wiltshire SN8 2HR

www.bhwesterns.com

Robert Hale is an imprint
of The Crowood Press

Typeset by
Derek Doyle & Associates, Shaw Heath
Printed and bound in Great Britain by
CPI Group (UK) Ltd, Croydon, CR0 4YY

CHAPTER ONE

Jubal Thorne was ploughing the field before the bullet went singing past his head. More truthfully, he was guiding his ox, Buddy, who was doing the actual pulling. Just the same, it was hard work keeping such a big animal on track, guiding that creature with a friendly word here and a sharp command there, hand on the enormous wooden yoke that the animal wore around his neck to transmit the power of those well-muscled shoulders to the plough. The plough itself was mostly made of wood, with a sharp curved metal blade at the front that cut through the rich soil as if it was snow.

Before the bullet and his day – no, days ahead – got much worse, Jubal was already hoping that he was elsewhere. It was hard work guiding the ox and he was already wet with perspiration. He wore loose black trousers held up with leather braces. His shirt was light with darker stripes, while his feet were clad in gumboots to help traverse the stiff clods of earth.

So far he could have been a sodbuster on any of countless farms, with his black, wide-brimmed hat jammed on his head. This just happened to be Oasis Valley, in Yuma County, Arizona, a valley fed by a tributary of the mighty Colorado, the silt from the river providing a richness of growth mostly missing from other counties in the territory.

It was the face below that brim an observer would have found striking. The right hand side was perfectly formed, handsome even, a man who could have been in his late thirties. Across an uneven line the left side degenerated into a melted mask with lines and scars on the uneven features. Over the sunken orbit on that side he wore a large dark-green leather patch to conceal the eye. His long, coppery hair hung in such a way as to partially conceal his face.

The reason he wanted to be elsewhere had nothing to do with hard work. He didn't mind that and plenty of it too. No, what affected him was the thought of the farm itself. It was just over twenty acres in size with fields in which big red potatoes, corn and squash grew readily enough.

But to Jubal, being here was as good as getting a jail sentence with no remission for good behaviour. He spoke his thoughts aloud to Buddy without the least hint of self-consciousness.

'Buddy, why did Frank have to die? I know he was older, and so on, but that son of a gun had a few more years left in him.' The ox grunted and strained at the yoke, the big black valley flies buzzing around him, while the soil broke open with a soft sigh as the blade of the plough parted it with implacable ease. Otherwise Jubal's words just hung in empty air.

'If it hadn't been for the loss of Belle and the little one he'd have had someone to carry on for him. As it is every day's the same.' He could not keep a trace of bitterness from his voice. Just the same, he knew that he could not have done otherwise. The story was simple enough. His brother, Frank, had been found dead on the outskirts of town by one of the local deputies, his horse beside him.

The local doc had come to have a look. But Frank, who was barely fifty, had succumbed to what looked like a heart attack. Jubal just happened to be in the area following his old profession – they called it being a bounty hunter in these parts – and news travels fast in a county. He rode into town as soon as he found out the grim news. The first time he had seen his brother for years was when Frank was already in his coffin.

Jubal could remember that when he was riding into Earlstown on his dark-coloured horse, Spirit, his first impression of the place was of a solidly built burgh. All the more remarkable when he knew thirty years before, this had been where a shanty town devoted to mining had stood. In those days it consisted mostly of canvas tents and hastily built ramshackle dwellings with tin roofs. The name Jackson Earl came to mind. He was the founder of Earlstown, justified in giving his name to the original dump because he had purchased all the claims. Earl had established a mine of a substantial size just outside town to dig out the remaining gold. Then, when that vein petered out he had turned to mining silver, which they had been doing ever since.

The town was bigger than ever because it was now part of the Great Western cattle trail that was just being established about the time Earl had his great vision of uniting the mines. Because of the regular influx of visitors Main Street held several saloons in various states of repair – ranging from the plush Gold Rush saloon, to the Grand, which was anything but. There was also a low building made of adobe and wood away from the other saloons that did not actually have a sign, except for the skull of a longhorn nailed to the front, which was a low drinking den where the primary attractions were cheap booze and being left alone. Further on down the street – nearly at the end in fact – was the big new church. It was less than twenty years old with a stone tower and built in a fairly basic manner. But it was painted white and green with green shutters to cover the plainer windows, and one large stained glass window. This showed one of the Lord's many acts, and overlooked the body of the church, positioned in such a way as to catch the rays of the evening sun.

At the service held there for his brother he had met Jackson Earl himself, his pretty wife and two lovely daughters. The founder, coming out of the church, had struck him as a particularly jovial kind of man, now in his late fifties, who immediately grasped Jubal's hand in commiseration.

'Mighty sorry to hear about your brother, he was a good man. But looking at the practical side, guess you'll be selling the farm?'

'No, reckon I'll settle down for a while. Could do with a rest.' Jubal noted how the jovial grin faded rapidly.

'Well think it over.' Then Earl was gone too.

Back at the ploughing, Thorne was thinking so much about his brother that he nearly ignored the tingle that went along his spine and raised the hairs at the back of his neck. If he had been thinking at all he might have reacted more slowly when the shot zitted past his head and there would be nothing else to tell. But his body was wiser than its owner, and he flung away and to the other side of the ox before he even knew what he was doing. As he moved swiftly away from the spot in which he had been standing barely a second before, his hands reached for the guns that should have been at his side, handles turned outwards for ease of use. Nothing: his fingers encountered only empty air.

His instincts had not betrayed him. Even as he ran he heard the sound of another bullet buzzing past his head like some demented insect. The boots that had carried him away were clumsy compared to those he had used when exercising his previous profession. Even so he moved with a swiftness and grace that belied the plodding of just a moment before.

The mountain of flesh beside him did not prove to be the safe haven it might have promised. Buddy gave a loud bellow, expelled a lot of air out of his lungs and keeled over in the direction of the man whose life he had inadvertently saved. The big yoke, the blade of the plough and most of all the potentially bone-crushing weight of the animal all began to come down upon him. He was saved once more by his reactions, and without thinking he managed to roll out of the way of the dying animal and somehow avoided being caught by the metal blade that could have sliced into his legs.

He was still on the ground, covered in fresh, damp soil when he saw the light fade out of the eyes of the animal. Thorne was not a sentimental man, he could not afford to be given his previous profession, but when he saw a harmless animal die, having taken a bullet for him, he felt the old fury rise inside him.

But he could not afford to lie in the field. Merely by changing vantage point, the killer in the woods beyond would be able to get an angle on the body of his or her prey, namely the ex-bounty hunter who was lying there covered in the mud he had helped to create.

Thorne was not stupid enough to get to his feet immediately. Instead he rolled over until he was beside the main body of the plough, the wooden structure at least offering a token defence, heaved to his feet and began to run towards the edge of the field. This time another shot kicked up some dirt at his feet and it began to seem obvious that the would-be killer was going to get his man.

9

Thorne was not a willing victim. He was used to calculating probabilities. He kept his narrow body from being an obvious target by running in a low crouch, keeping his head down and zig-zagging as he moved, all of these factors meaning that he was harder to hit.

He was heading for a spot the killer might not know existed. This was an irrigation ditch that ran all the way along the side of the field so that decent amounts of water could be channelled to the crops. The ditch was about four feet deep, and so placed that it was hard to see along the line of the field. In effect, what happened next from the would-be killer's point of view was that his intended victim disappeared as if swallowed by thin air.

Thorne did not bother with thoughts of bullets now, the ditch was half-full of water and for a moment he was face downwards with the muddy liquid filling his nose, mouth and ears. Channelled in from the Mighty Colorado, the water was surprisingly cold and he felt what little air was left in his lungs leave with a whoosh. In that moment it crossed his mind that there would be a terrible irony in drowning somewhere in Arizona in a few feet of water, considering it was supposed to be one of the driest territories on record.

He solved the problem by turning over on to his back and taking in a great lungful of air. If the would-be killer was coming to get him, the former gunman was in real trouble. He could only hope that the attacker still clung to the hope of remaining unidentified, or would think that he had actually succeeded in plugging his victim. To the killer's eyes it would certainly look that way; some of the bullets had been terribly close.

He decided to remain where he was for a few minutes, purely to make sure that he was not being shot at. Or at least that was his thought on the matter before he saw a

10

dark figure looming over the side of the ditch. Thorne was still not finished; as soon as he saw that he was in the presence of another human being he snaked out a sinewy arm and gave a great heave. The figure tried to keep its balance, but slid down the banking and landed beside the waterlogged farmer.

Thorne grabbed the figure by the front of his jerkin and was about to unleash a flurry of blows on the upturned face of the man who had landed beside him when he heard an anguished cry.

'Boss, what is it? It's me, Brand, heard some shots, dropped what I was doin' to get here.'

Most men have the advantage of two eyes; Thorne's one remaining uncovered orb cleared and he saw that he was indeed looking at his younger companion. He grunted and let go of the garment he was still holding.

'About time too,' he grunted. 'Come on, let's get out of this here watery haven, I'm getting a mite chilly.'

CHAPTER TWO

The two men hastened to the side of the field that led to the homestead. There was sparse shelter here and Thorne took hold of Brand by the arm, leading him towards the deeper undergrowth further along.

'Boss, you're in a state,' said Brand, shaking the head of thick dark hair that he had inherited from the Red Indian side of his family. He was known as Firebrand to his own people, but when Thorne employed the half-breed he knew that such a name would not endear him to the people of the town so he had it shortened to the less threatening one his companion now used.

'Brand, you aren't such a pretty sight yourself, but at least you're armed. I just hope the water didn't affect your gun. A wash-and-brush-up can wait, considering I've just been shot at. Close thing too. Wonder they didn't fire in your direction.'

Together they walked around the edge of the field keeping concealed behind the bushes and pinion trees. It wasn't much in the way of concealment but they were both experienced at hiding – Thorne for professional purposes, and Brand because he was part Indian and had trained well in getting away from hostile parties of either race. Both whites and Indians had been against him in his time.

It didn't take them long to get to the other side. By that time Brand was holding his gun, but he handed something to Thorne that he took from a concealed leather sheath in the side of his boot. It was a black-handled knife with a blade that had a wicked gleam to it, showing that it was kept razor-sharp. The former bounty hunter had a bump of location that could track a shot to within inches so when the pair jumped forward he was certain they were on target. It was a pity, then, that the target turned out to be a clump of flattened goose-grass between two stout trees.

'Looks as though he wanted to get you, ran as soon as he didn't.'

'Shush.' Thorne held up a slim hand, and they both heard the sound of hoofs pounding away in the distance.

The ex-gunman was nothing if not thorough. He knew they would never have time to get out to the stony path that ran past the farm and see whom the horseman was, so he concentrated instead on the area around where they stood. It was surprising how clumsy people could be when they were in a hurry, but he found nothing.

'Come on,' he said, 'we'll keep a lookout when we come back.'

'Why, what's happening?'

'We've got a job to do.'

Together they went back to the farmhouse, where it took him less than ten minutes to get changed, putting an old tunic over his fresh clothes. He would let his muddy clothes dry then get a stiff brush and give them a thorough going over, which would take out the dried soil in the form of a brown dust. In the meantime he fetched a couple of knives that looked like the big brothers of the one owned by Brand, and returned to the field accompanied by his companion.

The Indian understood straight away what it was they had to do. Stripping the hide off a carcass the size of the ox was not the hardest job when you knew what you were doing. They simply took the plough away from his inert body then began to work together, pulling the corpse this way and that in unison as they completed the task.

Then they cut up the animal. There was a lot of meat on a creature the size of Buddy, and Thorne, who was a practical man, didn't intend to waste any. They had a smokehouse at the farm – a brick building with narrow slits at the top on either side to let out some of the excess build-up of heat. It had a door that was simply a rectangular piece of metal held in place by a bar across the front.

Luckily they had plenty of fuel because they had been stocking up for the winter months when the nights in the desert valley could be surprisingly bitter, and it wasn't long before the meat was bathed in wood-smoke. Once cooked for a few hours it would be salted down in sealed barrels and would last for months.

They stretched out the hide, treated it and pegged it down. Nothing went to waste in the world of farming. It would be used for making garments.

All the time they were working the older man and his younger friend kept a lookout for possible intruders. Taking no chances, Thorne wore his gun belt, which fitted him as comfortably as an old glove. At last they were satisfied with their work and went back to the homestead. They went into the building where they discovered that they were both famished. Brand automatically took on the role of cooking the beans and pork that they were going to eat for their dinner. He was a paid hand, the only one on the twenty acres, but he was one more than Frank, who had preferred being here alone after the death of his wife and child.

'Well,' said Thorne, 'guess this means a trip into town tomorrow to buy a new ox. Shame really, I figured we wouldn't be eating old Buddy for a while yet. You stay here, Brand, and if there's any trouble shoot first and ask questions later.'

That was when they both heard the noise at the kitchen door, behind which they both stood. Thorne did not hesitate, but drew out his gun and threw the door open with his left hand, ready to defend what was his to the death if necessary.

Instead of some murderous intruder intent on taking his life, he found he was pointing his weapon at a young woman and two little girls. The three of them looked as startled as he felt.

CHAPTER THREE

'Can I help you?' Asked Thorne lamely.

'Perhaps you can Mr Thorne,' said the woman. 'I'm Agnes Greene and these are my girls, Sophie and Lauren. Can I speak to you please? In private.' She looked pointedly at the other man, who gave a quick nod of his dark head and went off with his plate into another part of the building. 'Girls, I want you to do me a favour,' said their mother. 'Go and play over there on the straw, just don't get yourselves dirty, and keep in sight.' The two girls, pretty little things both under seven years old, with blonde hair like their mother and chubby little bodies, did as they were asked and the distant sounds of their laughter soon filled the air. 'You know who I am,' she said, 'so I won't bother with any introductions.'

'We met at my brother's funeral if I remember correctly,' said Jubal. 'Would you come in? There's hot food and coffee.'

'We met again if you remember, at Donald's funeral, just last week.' Agnes Greene suddenly burst into tears and wiped her face with a cotton handkerchief removed from her sleeve. He had a feeling she had been crying a lot.

'Come in.'

'No, I have to keep an eye on the girls.'

'That was a bad business, a terrible accident.' He shook his head. 'To lose his life down a ravine like that.'

'He was killed,' said Agnes bluntly. She was in her late twenties, and quite pretty but there was an air of sadness about her, mixed with determination that she would be heard.

'I'm not sure if I know what to say.'

'I'm saying it all. He was killed, deliberately, by a person or people unknown and I'm still grieving.'

'Listen, if its money, I can help you out a little. We farming folk have to stick together.'

'It's nothing to do with money. We're not rich, but we'll get by. It's about justice. My husband was murdered and I want to find his killer and see him hanged. The Bible says an eye for an eye.' She burst into tears again.

While keeping a discreet silence as she wiped her face, Thorne thought over what was supposed to have happened. Donald Greene had been riding home when his horse, it was said, had stumbled and pitched him into a ravine just outside the valley called Dead Man's Ravine. Ironic really, but of course no one dared say it. His wife had been expecting him and when he hadn't turned up, she had ridden out to meet him and found the body. It seemed as common an accident as any. People were killed quite often in this uneven territory in this kind of incident, taking their steeds for granted. In her grief, it seemed she would not accept what had really happened.

'So who do you think could have been responsible for such a thing?' he asked.

'First of all, I want to ask you a question. What are you?'

'I don't know how to answer that question,' he said, taken a little aback by her directness. When he had first met Agnes she had seemed a pretty but mousy little thing, a woman of little substance, now she turned out to have the fierce qualities of a real pioneer woman.

'I've heard the stories,' she said. 'I know that you've been a man who has faced danger. Most people turn and run at the first sign of trouble, but not you. You've stood up to the bad men and you've come through. Would you stand up for me? I've got some money if that's what you need, our savings.'

'You haven't answered my question. Who would have done this?'

'I don't know really. What about Jackson Earl? How's about those thugs who lounge about and act as if they own the place, led by that oaf Bug Lannigan? Then there's that creepy undertaker Pate Hardin. He makes my skin crawl and not just because of his profession, and he's in with the mayor, and owner of the town, who's also Earl. Finally – and I mean this – there's that Morton Bradley, who treated me as if I was insane when I told him I thought Donald was much too good a rider to fall down a ravine like that. He, Bradley, dismissed the whole thing. I helped lay out the body, I used to be a nurse. I'm telling you, some of those injuries were of a man who was beaten up before going down there.'

Privately Thorne considered that Bradley, the sheriff, might be quite right, that he was dealing with a faintly unhinged woman who would just not accept that her husband had died in an accident caused by inattention and riding too fast, but he did not want to distress her any further.

'Ma'am, I would love to help you,' he said, 'but as far as I can see you don't have a scrap of evidence against anyone. There's another factor you haven't taken into account. I've led a colourful life; I won't hesitate to admit that truth. I've even killed a few men in my time; I won't deny that fact either. But I saw what happened to my brother. How he built up this business from scratch. I took over because if I didn't all this would be lost. 'Sides a man gets tired of being on the trail, and the heat and the killing. I'm settled here, and I don't want to rile a whole town against me.'

'In other words you're not going to help me,' she said flatly, her green eyes searching his one exposed orb for confirmation.

'I never said that.'

'But that's what you meant, and as for your little speech, it sounds to me as if you're spending a mighty long time convincing yourself that what you've done is OK, but you're a restless man Mr Thorne, and that restlessness will win, you'll see.' She backed away from the door.

'Wait, where are you going?'

'It's all business,' she said. 'Wait until they come knocking on your door and try and take it all away from you. Just one more thing – Donald was under pressure to sell the farm to unspecified buyers through that slippery lawyer, Spendlow. Those buyers want our land.'

'Wait, come on and talk.'

'No, you've made up your mind. I'll fight my own cause now. Come on girls,' she called across the yard, gathering her children and marching off to where her buggy and pair waited outside the yard. Thorne watched her go and shook his head as he went back inside and took up his now cold meal.

CHAPTER FOUR

Thorne rode into town the next day. He was feeling a bit tired because he had been up half the night patrolling the border and the precincts of his own farm. The rest of the watch had been taken by Brand, who still remained behind for the simple reason that the work of a farm had to continue. Crops still had to be planted, animals still had to be tended, and equipment maintained. There was one crucial difference to his bearing. He was armed now with his trusty weapon, a single long-nosed Peacemaker with a greater range than the average handgun. The handle was worn, showing that it had been used a great deal, although it kept its secrets about where and when. To him, this one, and the partner weapon he had left at home, were almost living objects that he would strip and reassemble and keep in good working order as a matter of course.

It was still early in the morning, although not early enough to see the miners going off to work with their spades or picks carried on their shoulders. He did not envy them their work. Not only that, their living conditions never seemed to get any better and most of them lived in shacks or adobe dwellings on the edge of town nearest the mines, which made good sense since this involved only a short walk to work.

Although still early, there was a pulse of warmth in the air that indicated that this was going to be a hot, dusty day in Earlstown. Thorne was glad he had arrived here early; he had a few business transactions to complete, not the least of which involved an engagement with the law.

Morton Bradley, the sheriff, was seated on the porch outside his office, chair tilted back against the wooden side of the building as he enjoyed the last dregs of his morning coffee from the blue tin mug that was used all the time and barely washed. He flung the dregs to one side, on the soil, as Thorne dismounted and came forward leading Spirit.

'How do Sheriff Bradley, can a man have a word with you?'

'Sure can,' said the sheriff, 'that's what I'm here for. 'Sides I've plenty time, it's mid-week and there ain't a cowboy in my cells yet.'

'You may have cause to give some other *hombre* a space when I ask for your involvement,' said Thorne easily.

'Yeah? Well tell all.' The sheriff lit a roll-up and stayed seated.

'Some ambitious hustler decided to take a shot at me yesterday – not just one, but two – darn near got me too, but luckily these old legs went into automatic mode and I got out of there pretty fast. Didn't get me, but killed my ox and he was pretty essential for keeping the fields ploughed.'

The sheriff was quite young, but he smoked his cigarette thoughtfully like a much older man, taking long draws and blowing out a plume of smoke, eyes narrowed as he considered the matter.

'Did you see anyone at the time?'

'No, just found some tracks.'

'Where did they lead to?'

'They were on vegetation; by the time we got back to looking whoever did the deed was long gone.'

'Then I'm mighty sorry for the loss of your animal, but there's nothing I can do.'

'Would you like to come out for a look-see?'

'I'll send out one of my deputies later, seems to me there's not a lot I can do.'

'A man nearly gets killed just a mile or two away and you don't seem that interested.'

'Let's get something clear Mr Thorne,' Bradley got lazily to his feet and threw away the last of his roll-up. 'I was sworn in to protect the citizens of this here town, that's about the remit for me. Seems to me what you've got here is what I calls a lazy protest.'

'What do you mean mister?'

'I mean that some disgruntled settler gets himself a gun and decided that he's going to wreak a little revenge on some man, not any particular man, just the first one he comes across.'

'Why do you reckon that, Sheriff Bradley?'

'Because, Mr Thorne, others made claim on this valley long before the rest of us, that's why. Now and then some poor ornery tramp gets likkered up on illegal hooch and comes out looking for a little revenge.'

'I guess you got the rights of most what happened,' said Thorne, 'but I was there and it didn't feel like a few random drunken shots to me. Felt like I was a chosen target.'

'And as I say, this place was once a mining camp, now it's a good part of the cattle trail. After the long walk through the desert they come here and use the meadows around town to water and fatten their beasts. Every weekend without fail I have to go in and bust up fights in the saloons or deal with shootings right here and organize the odd hanging, summary justice if you get my drift.' His eyes strayed to a wooden beam that jutted out from the roof of the jail and Thorne understood at once its dreadful purpose.

'Besides, I heard you ain't averse to employing some Indian help yourself, Mr Thorne.'

'Why not? Brand is the hardest worker I've ever known.'

'No reason at all, but just watch your back. Them half-breeds is dangerous kittle, don't know which ways they belong.' The sheriff gave a smile that made him seem much younger although he was in his thirties. 'Been a pleasure talking to you Mr Thorne, and I'll get one of my deputies to check out this business.'

'Just like you checked out the death of Donald Greene?'

'That was an accident, plain and simple. His horse pulled up too hard and he broke his neck down a ravine. It happens.' The sheriff narrowed his eyes as he looked at the man who purported to be a farmer. 'Just remember this, mister, I don't tolerate anyone who wants to cause trouble in this here town.'

'I'll remember, just as much as I'll recall how much help I got here today.'

'That suits me fine. I'll let you get on with your day.' Bradley tilted his chair against the wall and tipped his hat over his eyes.

Thorne did not take his dismissal particularly hard. He was too busy to hold any grudges. But what he did want to do was sound out some of the locals on their thinking about the death of Donald Greene. But he was more than a little curious to see if he could figure out who had wanted him dead as well. The good side of his face hardened at the thought while the other side remained an expressionless mask. If it was a fight someone or unknown someones wanted, he was their man.

He was leading his horse down Main Street when he came to the burnt-out shell of what had been a fairly small building that had once stood apart from the businesses on either side. A sign above the warped door proclaimed that this had once been '*The Town Crier*, Prop. H. Jones.' This fact alone told him that all was not well with the town. He tied Spirit to a rail outside the Gold Rush, and Spirit gratefully dipped his head in the half-full trough, while his owner went to have a look at the wrecked building. An elderly man wearing shapeless black trousers and a grey shirt was walking past and he saw Thorne looking at the defunct newspaper office. He stopped and looked at the stranger.

'Pretty sight ain't it?' asked the man.

'I guess not,' said Thorne.

'Name is Tomms,' said the man, who had several days' growth of white whiskers and wasn't as old as he had seemed on first sight. 'Joseph Tomms, uster be a miner but this old frame's too broke for that. Still live with my son though, over the back.' He indicated the direction of the miners' houses, a motley collection of buildings away from the main town, some of which had been part of the original mining camp. 'You're the dude who took over from Frank. He was a good guy, uster slip us a dollar now and then. Bad business this altogether, nobody knows who did it. Old Jonsey, he's never recovered, he drinks now.'

'In there?' Thorne jerked his head in the direction of the Gold Rush.

'Naw, he drinks in the same spot as the rest of us, me and other fellers who got too unfit ta work, down in the 'Skull as we calls it.'

'Does he say what happened to his business?'

'He don't say nothing, just crawls inside a bottle and

stays there.' Thorne shrugged. It didn't really matter. He had enough trouble in his own life without having to look into what had happened to other people. But the old miner's next words made him lift his head.

'Reckon it might have been to do with the stuff he was printing and all.'

'In what way?'

'About people in this town and all that.' The ex-miner looked around nervously. 'Ain't good to talk too loud about this kind of stuff in this part of town.'

Thorne saw that Tomms was looking further down the street. Thorne turned and saw that four men were walking along the dusty road in a group, swaggering a little, moving with the gait of men who were more used to walking than riding horses now, used to employing their own feet for locomotion. Thorne did not know the other three, but he recognized their leader, Bug Lannigan, who had been in the background the day he had first met Jackson Earl, the day of his brother's funeral.

'Pine, Clarke and Binns,' said Tomms, 'a worse case you never saw of people ris above their station.'

'Who are they?'

'Just a bunch of fellers who think they have a right to lord it over the rest of us. Wouldn't think to look at them they was just miners like the rest of us at one time. That Bug's the worse.' The elderly man bowed his head and looked a little frightened. Thorne did not waste any more time, but produced a silver dollar and flung it to him.

'Got to keep up a family tradition.' The old man caught it and thrust it into a trouser pocket without any hesitation.

Bug came within speaking distance and halted, legs spread wide. He was dressed like a cowboy, with a wide-brimmed black hat, a dark waistcoat with a blue shirt beneath and a pair of blue jeans. His men were dressed in a similar manner, although to Jubal Thorne's experienced eye the four were too well-fed, clean and sleek-looking to be true riders. He did not much like those who pretended to be something they were not. The guns holstered at their sides were real enough, though. Thorne judged that they were all carrying Smith & Wessons, none particularly modified, except for the one carried by their leader, which had a silver handle indicating that he had some kind of good, regular income to afford such a fancy modification.

Bug Lannigan had a wide Slavic-looking face and a downward curve to his mouth that indicated he did a lot of sneering. The curve of his mouth was accentuated by his thick black moustache. He was sneering now with faint contempt as he looked at the farmer and the elderly miner. His skin was somewhat reddened, whether by the fierce sun or drink it was impossible to say; perhaps a combination of both.

'Having a good day boys?'

'Just goin',' said Tomms, backing away so hastily that he tripped over his own feet, stumbled badly and would have fallen if not for a restraining hand from his companion. The four men laughed, more so when Tomms pulled away from Jubal and made off down the dusty street as fast as his arthritic feet could carry him.

'Real funny,' said Thorne as he turned his gaze back to the four men. He noticed that the other three did not carry their presence with quite the same boldness as their leader, but they would attack soon enough at Bug's command. Every pack had to have a lead wolf. He liked that lack of confidence he saw in them, because he knew that despite the way they were standing in pale imitation of their leader, at heart they were really just the miners they had always been.

Thorne inwardly cursed the fact that he had only one weapon at his hip today. With two guns he could take them all, but with one he was a sitting target, all due to the time factor. With two guns he could take two out at once.

'So,' said Lannigan easily, 'you come to town.'

'I'm here on business.'

'Well it sure looks to me as if you're taking a long time with the matter, hob-nobbing with locals and the like.'

'Well you know what it's like, being new to the territory, settling down, just putting out a few feelers.'

'So that's why you spoke to the old-timer?'

'Fact is, he spoke to me, not the other way about. Not that it matters in any case, because I can talk to whoever I want.'

'This one's a bit uppity,' said the one called Binns. 'Do you think we should teach him a lesson, boss – maybe kick up a little bullet dust at his feet, make him do one of them dance routines?' The man who spoke was taller and weedier than Lannigan. He had a weak chin and a big nose.

'Easy Binns,' said Lannigan, putting out a restraining hand. 'Mr Thorne here is moving on real soon, going back to the farm.'

'With the pigs, where he belongs,' snickered another of the men.

'I told you, Clarke, you don't get an opinion right now,' said Lannigan. 'Reckon Mr Thorne here ain't the farming type, he'll get fed up real quick and let the property go to someone who makes him a reasonable offer. Ain't that right Mr Thorne?'

'Are you asking me or telling me?' asked Thorne.

'Not saying a lot, just making conversation,' said Lannigan. He leapt forward suddenly and a less controlled man might have jumped, but Jubal did not so much as

27

twitch a muscle as Lannigan, followed by his men, marched past and trooped up the three steps to the board-walk, pushing forward the batwing doors that led into the saloon. As he entered the building Lannigan spoke in a loud voice but without as much as a backward glance.

'We'll just wet our tubes, when we come out the sour-puss will be well gone.'

Jubal Thorne knew when he was being threatened. He also knew that he had done the right thing in not backing down. With that type, once they thought they had put you in your place they just took it as a sign that they could take even more liberties.

He was not finished; before he went to buy another ox he had someone to see. The road curved round towards where the old man had gone. Thorne could see the low, mostly adobe building quite a bit further on. It had the skull of a longhorn nailed to the front and looked about the lowest kind of drinking establishment you could get. Main Street was like that, a strange mix of brand new saloons like the Gold Rush, a smart hotel, a church, all intermixed with remnants of the old mining town. A modern-looking shop front confronted him. This was one business that was not in the habit of selling goods, but rather of taking them in. This was the shop front of Pater Hardin, funeral director.

A bell tinkled as Thorne entered. His sensitive nostrils were immediately assailed by the rich scent of pine resin, waxy candles and a subtle but cloying smell that caught faintly in the back of the throat and was actually the sweet smell of decaying flesh. Bodies didn't keep too well in this kind of climate and funerals tended to occur pretty quickly after the demise of whoever had gone to meet their maker.

The front shop was plain enough, undecorated walls

painted with distemper, an oak desk and chair in the corner for writing details of the deceased, and another, wider doorway that he guessed would lead into the funeral parlour where those who were so disposed could view the body. There was barely a pause, and then Pater Hardin, the undertaker, came through this second door with an expectant look on his features that quickly faded when he saw his new visitor.

'Mr Thorne, how can I help you?'

'Just wanted a few words about one of your clients.'

'You'd better come with me.' Hardin led him into the funeral parlour. There was an open pine coffin with a young woman in it. He hastily closed the lid. 'Sorry, her family are due for a viewing. Childbirth death, very sad. Now is it about your brother's headstone? It's nearly ready, sorry that it's been over a month, but I don't make them you know. I have a monumental sculptor for that kind of thing, but he's had a lot of work to do.' As he spoke the dark-clothed man rubbed his hands together out of pure habit and spoke in a low voice that barely rose above a murmur. He seemed very quiet and respectful but there was something sly about the man that Thorne did not like. And not just because of his profession.

'It's nothing to do with that. I know these things take time and Frank wouldn't have minded. He would have asked not to have one, would've called it a waste of money. No, I want a word about Donald Greene.'

Was it his imagination or did a look of alarm pass across the undertaker's sallow features? If so it was an emotion that was swiftly repressed.

'I'm not sure I can help. His coffin was oak, you know, one of the best. Pine is far cheaper.'

'I just need to know something. When his body came to you did you notice anything unusual about his injuries? Or

29

were they what you would have expected from that kind of fall?'

'Let me say this to you, sir, that I have seen a lot of bodies in my time. At this pass it can be hard for me to remember details, but yes, yes, that particular demise was sad and recent.'

'So what can you tell me?'

'I can only say that the fall caused a lot of damage, contusions, and a broken neck.' The undertaker narrowed his eyes. 'I sense this has nothing to do with you, really. You are Agnes Greene's neighbour, aren't you?' He noted the way Thorne said nothing but shifted a little uncomfortably. 'Agnes has never accepted that he died in an accident. She was hysterical at the funeral. Now she's spreading this nonsense again. You, sir, I would advise you to keep your nose out of this business. She is not in a stable frame of mind.'

'You still haven't answered my question.'

'Of course it was accidental, I've seen men shot, beaten or dead from heart attacks, this was a classic steep fall.'

'Thanks, that's all I needed to know.'

The undertaker indicated the way out with the flat of his hand and led Jubal into the front shop. Thorne turned to face Hardin.

'Thanks for your help, you'll be in touch about that headstone?'

As he was speaking, the shop door tinkled as it swung open; there was a tread of heavy feet, then a big hand grabbed him by the shoulder. This was a mistake for that person to make. Thorne was already on edge from his earlier conversation with Lannigan and in his mind the thug had tracked him down and was about to commit some act of violence against his would-be victim.

Thorne tore away from the other's grasp so violently

that he almost collided with the undertaker, who had to take a step backwards. As he pulled away Thorne turned, Peacemaker Colt in his hand as if by some miracle, so flowing had been his draw that it had not actually been visible to the naked eye.

He crouched beside the desk in the corner and faced the newcomer, ready to use the weapon, his face grim as death.

CHAPTER FIVE

As he crouched there and looked up at the new arrival, Thorne found that he was gazing into the startled features of Albert J. Spendlow, lawyer at large. The lawyer was a big man who belied the view that lawyers were generally hawk-like seekers after truth on behalf of their clients. Spendlow had an avuncular manner about him and wore a linen suit, a tailored shirt and a dark tie. In one hand was the fedora he had taken off on entry, revealing his almost totally bald head. His even features were pleasant enough once they lost their look of astonishment, then he had the grace to laugh.

'Well partner, looks like you got the drop on me.'

'Beg pardon,' said Thorne as he stood upright and holstered his gun. 'Been a bit jumpy lately is all. Thanks for your help Pater, there's some things a man needs to know.' He made his way out into the dusty street. He was not the least bit bothered about drawing a bead on the lawyer. Spendlow was a big shot here, but he was pretty small fry in the world beyond and Thorne had seen a great deal of that world. Neither did he think it strange that the lawyer and undertaker seemed to be good friends – he had seen the looks they exchanged after his faux pas – he knew well enough that where there was a corpse there was often an estate and it didn't take much for a family to be at each other's throats over one detail or another. He had once seen two men fall out with one another over who was to inherit their brother's six guns. The dispute was settled when one of the brothers took it in his head to use said guns to end the dispute with a bang. He was sentenced and hanged. The guns went to the county auction.

Standing where he was, his eye was caught by a land-mark that he really should have noticed before. The terrain behind the town was somewhat rocky, and there on a hill behind the mixture of buildings that was Earlstown, stood a mansion high on the hill. The town had other good houses where the professional classes stayed, but these shrank into insignificance compared with the build-ing that now caught his gaze. It was mostly a gaze of puzzlement, because if truth be told, the magnificent edifice might not have been out of place in a prosperous city like Boston, but here it was as freakish as a golden shell on a snail. Without even being told he knew that this must be the home of Jackson Earl. Instead of tucking his earnings from the mines away, he had clearly decided that he was going to make a great show of his opulence.

Thorne felt a little stab of resentment at the sight, not because he was envious of the wealth accrued by the mine owner, but in comparison to the mean little shacks his workers lived in, the mansion, which had an east wing and more windows than you could count, was a palace. To Thorne it was like a slap in the face to those who had laboured hard to put Earl into that house on the hill, and that didn't just include the miners, but those who had done the back-breaking work of building such a place in this remote location. The stonework alone must have cost a fortune.

Looking at the wide road from the mansion that swept

into town, Thorne knew that he was in the presence of Western royalty. No wonder the man had brought his opulence to this part of town; these were his subjects to command and he wanted that power. Thorne had seen men with more money than they knew what to do with before, the strange paradox being that most of them were less happy than when they were struggling to make the money in the first place.

He had little time to waste in mere sightseeing; indeed he had wasted enough of his day making enquiries about Agnes Greene's dead spouse, now it was time to get on with his own work.

He went to the market, negotiated a fair price and bought an ox for the ploughing work. An ox is a splendid animal, built for strength, but does not have the greatest turn of speed so it was early afternoon before he was back at the farm.

'Seen anything?' he asked Brand on his return. The Indian knew exactly what he was being asked.

'No sign of anyone boss,' he said cheerfully. 'Looks like we're safe after all.'

'Not so sure about that,' said Jubal, 'though the sheriff says it sounds like the work of some half-breed renegade.' He allowed a smile to play on his lips as he said this. Brand gave a shout of laughter. He was far different from the surly boy Thorne had hired as his sidekick a couple of years before. He was no longer a hired hand, more like a confidante in the midst of the madness that Thorne had gone through in the last few years. Brand even revelled in being a farm worker. He enjoyed looking after the animals, including the pigs and horses, and he was allowed to be with someone who did not judge him by his race.

'If I had wanted you dead, you'd have been dead.'

'I guess so. Anyway the shots were from the wrong direction.'

This settled, Thorne spent the next few days being busy on the farm. This was not hard to do, because they were behind with ploughing the fields so the young ox, once he was broken in, soon found out what hard work was like. He did not seem to particularly mind this, especially as his new master, who knew the value of these things, kept him well fed and watered.

Once the fields were ready, the crop had to be sowed using a seed drill and both Thorne and Brand worked overtime to get this done. Eventually he would be able to harvest, amongst other crops, corn, squash and potatoes. It was not as if he did not have a market for these things because they would sell in the town and beyond.

All the time he was working the thought of Agnes was in the back of his mind, and he kept meaning to go and see her, but one day seemed to merge into another and he would see her when he was not as busy.

A couple of weeks raced by in this manner.

One night, after a particularly hard day of back-breaking work he crawled into bed and was dead to the world almost at once. Then, in the midst of what was a moonlit night, he had a horrible dream where he could feel that warning tingle down his spine and he could hear distant shouts and hoof beats but there was nothing he could do because he was completely paralysed. It was many years since he had suffered the events that led to the present condition of his face, but after what had happened to him then, he had experienced precisely the same symptoms. He awoke and sat up in bed. He had a wind-up clock beside him just to tell the time of day, not as an alarm because he always awoke at precisely six in the morning, especially since he had cut down on his drinking.

There was a fine sheen of sweat on his forehead and the moon was shining through the window upon his supine body, but there was no noise except for the chirruping of insects and the distant howls of a coyote to break the silence of the velvet night. Finally, after a restless half-hour he went back to sleep again and woke up a few hours later not wholly refreshed.

A couple of days later he had to go into town to get fresh supplies of seed and a couple of hand tools from the hardware store. As he stopped his buckboard in front of the building and tied up the horses, he was aware of a voice he recognized shouting his name. He got down from the front of the carriage and found that he was being hailed by Sheriff Bradley.

'How do?' asked Thorne.

'Howdy,' said the sheriff, 'thought I had better keep you up to date. Sent one of my deputies out to the edge of your farm to have a look-see. I guessed you would have done the same, and he found about as much as you did.'

'Which was precisely nothing.'

'Nothing except a lot of ploughed field and a good few bits of dug-over earth.'

'I don't know what the last is; maybe Brand was up to something.'

'Whoever tried to turn you into a colander was well and truly gone within minutes.'

'Well at least you tried to find out, even if you sent one of your boys because a possible shooting didn't merit the sheriff's attention.'

Jubal turned away, or at least began to do so, but the sheriff started forward.

'Wait, mister, I have other news. The deputy went to see Agnes, just to find out how she was getting on – besides, he was a bit nosy.'

'I've been meaning to see her,' Jubal. 'Pressure of work.'

'Well you won't be seeing her no more,' said the sheriff bluntly.

'How come?'

'Fact is, her home was open to the four winds and there was a note saying that she couldn't stand it here without her man. She says, in the note, that she's quit the whole darn business and gone to live with her family back in Tucson. Don't blame her neither, what with her being out there alone with them little mites.'

'Don't you think that seems a bit suspicious, that she should disappear like that without selling the property?'

'You didn't see her when her man first died. She was totally out of her mind with grief. She's been spreading wild stories, and she's been telling everyone how she wants to get out of here. The property was free to them when they first settled, anyhow, and she was definitely planning on going. Between us, I heard through the grapevine she withdrew her money from the bank just a few days before her disappearance.'

'Then I suppose that says it all.' Thorne gave a shrug of his lean shoulders. 'Guess all that I need to do is get on with my day. So what happens to her property now?'

'The town'll put in a claim.'

'I sure don't understand what you mean by that.'

'It's a local law; if a property lies unclaimed by an heir for thirty days after the owner dies or abandons it, the estate reverts back to the town as common property, then it can be purchased for a bargain price.'

'Doesn't seem too fair. So if I hadn't heard about my brother, in a month I wouldn't have been able to claim his farm?'

'That about sums it up.'

'But the town fathers would then be able to sell off the land and all the buildings on it? Seems a bit unjust, that's all.'

'You would think so Mr Thorne, but I guess you need to know a little bit of the history of this place before you make a judgement. You see in the early days, before I was even born, this was just a mining town with a lot of claims. People built where they wanted. Disease was rife and Indian attacks were frequent and brutal. Jackson Earl consolidated all the claims into one big one and he gave work to a lot of people. Then the government announced that if someone made a land claim they could come in and do so. Most of the free land was at the head of the valley and a lot of smallholders came in.'

'I find that hard to believe, a lot of the land is fallow right now.'

'In them days it was hard to get the equipment needed to farm, and a lot of families struggled and failed. At one time a lot of smallholdings were abandoned and lay empty, sometimes for years, and we've had droughts here, you know.'

Thorne could not argue with this. Even in times of good weather, farming the land was difficult, as his aching back could attest.

'We votes in sheriffs, mayors and all in this area, so the vote was cast that land should revert to the town and a fresh claim could be made. It means the land owner gets a bargain and the town gets money in its coffers.'

'While the lawyer and the mayor get to swell their bank accounts, not to mention the man on the hill, who just happens to be the mayor.'

'That's dangerous talk Thorne, I'd keep it to yourself. Now what about your own little problem?' The sheriff looked faintly hostile at the turn the conversation had taken, not looking that concerned for Thorne, as if he was duty bound to ask the question.

'Nothing, I've been left alone.'

'There you are, I told you it was just some maverick taking it out on an easy target.'

'Well, I'll get on with my day,' said Thorne. 'Looks as if everything worked out OK for all concerned.'

'Looks that way.'

The two men parted and Thorne went for his hardware as planned; a good axe, nails, a new blade for the bow saw, and other sundries. At first he did not think too much about his neighbour. The matter was, as he had agreed with the sheriff, settled. But there was one aspect that Bradley had not taken into consideration. Agnes Greene had turned to Thorne for help and he had let her down. The former gunman had every excuse for doing so, and he had been busy since, but the fact was, he had done nothing for her. He had been too ready to accept answers about what had really happened. In fact, when he examined the matter, her departure settled a lot of issues, unanswered questions, some of which he himself had raised. The truth was that it was in everyone's interest, including his own, to stop his enquiries and get on with the job in hand. He had plenty of work ahead, including keeping his crops free of pests, the eventual harvest and selling his produce when the time came. He should dismiss her from his mind.

So far it had just been a day like any other. That was about to change.

As he finished loading the last of his goods on to the buckboard he saw some familiar figures swaggering down the street towards him; Lannigan and his three shadows. Thorne was still standing there beside his horses when Lannigan strolled over.

'Say, if it ain't old one-eye. You took our warning serious then? You sure haven't been around awhile.'

'I come into town and leave when I want,' said Thorne evenly. The three men were crowding forward along with Lannigan. Thorne stepped back and stumbled as his heel caught the edge of the boardwalk. He stepped up as the four burst forth with more laughter than was merited by the act.

'You're a clumsy galoot,' said Lannigan. 'Sure you oughter be doing your job? Seems to me it's easy for a man to have a bad accident when he's as clumsy as you.'

'Could be,' said Thorne laconically. With one easy motion he got into the seat behind his horses. He did not waste any more words but gave his reins a crack and the animals started forward, so that the men had to fall back to the road. The town was busy and as Thorne departed, he heard some shouts of laughter from other walkers at their discomfort.

'Curse him,' shouted Binns, 'he got my foot with his damn wheel.'

'Shoulda been your head you stupid bastard,' said Lannigan with a notable lack of sympathy.

Thorne felt the spot between his shoulder blades itch but he rode on, ready to throw his body to one side at any moment, but no shot came.

For now.

He had met men like Lannigan before and he knew that if he stayed around, some kind of showdown was inevitable, but first he had to figure out why the ex-miner was leaning on him so hard, and the answers did not sit comfortably with him. He decided that this was a job to Lannigan, and if it was a job, there was an employer somewhere. He got home and unloaded the new tools with the help of Brand, who had been waiting for him.

'No work today except for feeding the animals,' said Thorne. The half-breed looked at him and waited for an answer to the question that he did not need to ask.

'You and me, we're going for a little ride,' said Thorne, 'out to the Greene place.' Brand did not ask why they were taking this step since it was not his habit to question why Thorne did anything. The answer always lay in the result, and Jubal was not a man who carried out an act without reason.

The other holding was reached via a trail down the side of the valley, and was far closer to Earlstown than Thorne's place. As they took to the trail there was a feeling of heat in the air that had not been there earlier. Thorne felt something akin to unease, but not for his own safety. As far as he was concerned, if he was physically challenged he had every right to retaliate and if there was some threat of the law going against him – as it had in other territories even though justice was on his side – well, they would have to catch him first.

His first impression of the Greene spread showed that it was not as well managed as his own. They had obviously had a few animals because he could see tracks, but most of these seemed to have been taken away or perhaps had wandered off when they were left to their own devices. A few sheep were contentedly chewing grass in a field, but the stables were empty. It looked, indeed, as if Agnes had taken the two horses they had and their buggy and had just set out to make the trip to Tucson with her two small children.

Then the ridiculous nature of the thought struck him. Even in her circumstances, surely she would have tried to sell the property before she went? It was a long trip and they would have needed quite a few supplies to get them there.

They dismounted from their horses and walked into the yard. Beyond a few outhouses lay the main farm building.

'You walk around the outside of the farmland,' said Thorne, 'they only had a few acres so it shouldn't take you too long.'

'What am I looking for?' Thorne did not hesitate on that one.

'Whatever you can see.' The Indian did not hesitate either, but got back on his horse and took off without another word.

Jubal was armed, but he kept his Peacemaker firmly in its holster as he approached the homestead. In stark contrast to some of the fine new townhouses to be found in Earlstown, it was a mean-looking building that must have been there long before the Greene family arrived and took over the land. The roof was covered in wooden shingles nailed in place. The entire building was little bigger than one of the outhouses and had small windows with wooden frames that were painted a dark shade of green. The front door was dark green with a wooden doorknob. Jubal hesitated and then turned this, crossing into the interior quickly, having to stoop a little as he did so.

The inside was as gloomy as he had imagined, and there was an unlit kerosene lamp sitting on an oak table in the front room, and a roomy fireplace. He found nothing there of any value, but he noted that the remnants of food – simple bread and meat – lay on a plate on the table. He would have thought that she would have taken any food with her. He went into the bedroom where he found from the spare cots that the children must have shared the same room as their parents. As for the note that she was supposed to have left, he saw no sign of this in either room so he supposed that it must have been given to Bradley, who had accepted the words at face value.

He took to thinking about Bradley. The man was straightforward enough in the way he spoke and acted, but was he working for the powers that be in more than his capacity as an elected functionary? The answer to that could be yes and no, according to the way you looked at it. Thorne realized he was going to have to see the sheriff again, soon, and annoy the hell out of him.

Hopefully Brand would use his tracking skills around the area and tell Jubal what he had discovered, maybe giving them a clue as to what had really happened to the missing woman.

Thorne thought he was alone in this area, so it was a minor shock when he stepped out of the building into the afternoon air to find that he was confronted with the very image of Agnes Greene. For a second he thought he was seeing a ghost, then he realized that the woman facing him now was much too young to be Agnes although she had the same even features and long, golden hair. She was also he noticed a fraction of a second later, holding a Colt 0.44 that was aimed straight at his heart.

'Mister,' she said, 'you're a dead man,' and she began to squeeze the trigger.

CHAPTER SIX

At the last second, the woman who looked so much like Agnes jerked her gun upwards and to one side. She fired the bullet up into the air, and the gun jumped in her hand like a live thing, while the roar of the bullet, that close, was enough to leave a ringing in their ears. Thorne tensed his muscles to jump at her and knock the weapon out of her hands.

'Let that be a lesson to you mister, now get right out of here and don't come on this land again.'

'I'm leaving,' said Thorne, keeping his voice level and holding his hands out in a gesture that seemed to placate her a little. 'I was just doing a little investigation. No harm done.'

'What were you investigating – friend?' asked the girl in a voice that was as fierce as her expression.

'I got so bound up in my own affairs that I didn't listen to a plea for help from a woman who looked pretty much like you. When I heard she wasn't around any more I decided to come to the farm and have a look for myself.'

'My sister? You spoke to her? When?'

'I'm afraid it was a couple of weeks ago. She was really asking me for help and I just brushed the whole matter aside.' He was not a man to sweeten the blunt truth, especially when he was feeling bad about the matter.

'So who are you? What's your name?'

'I could ask you the same thing. Mind you, it's easier having a conversation with another party when you don't have a gun pointing at your face. Especially when your hands are trembling so much that it's liable to go off again.'

'Mister, as far as I'm concerned you're just a stranger on my brother-in-law's land. You could be saying anything. Besides, you don't look like a farmer to me; you look like some man who's been out on the range for a considerable part of his life.'

'That's the truth of the matter miss, but I'm a farmer now. Jubal's the name, Jubal Thorne.'

'See I guessed they would send somebody, or bodies, to evict me now my sister's gone, especially when I learned what I was told in town. I just didn't expect it to happen so soon.' Then her eyes widened as his words hit her more fully. 'Wait a moment – your face, I never noticed before in the shadow and the way its part hidden by your hair, and that name, Thorne, I've heard it before. You're some kind of bounty hunter, a hired killer.' Beads of sweat appeared on her brow and she tightened her grip on the butt of the weapon.

'Well sister, let me put you straight on that one. I might have been a bounty hunter, but I'm no hired hand, and I've settled down on Frank's old holding. It's mine now I guess.'

'So you knew Frank? I heard my sister speak of him, he was a good man, did a lot for her and Donald in the early days.'

'He was my brother.'

She studied his face long and hard for what seemed like

an eternity before finally lowering her gun.

'My name's Annie, and I hope I haven't made the worst mistake of my life.'

'That's better.' He had kept his voice as relaxed as possible, but he had not relished the proximity of the weapon. What she had not known was that he had been quite capable of taking the gun from her for the last few minutes, but he had stopped his impulse towards doing this because he wanted to know more about her.

'I'm Annie Bateman,' she said, brushing a tendril of strawberry blonde hair away from her mouth. 'Like I said, I thought you might be them.'

'In this case,' said Thorne, 'it would be a great help if you defined who "they" are.'

'It's like this. As you know Earlstown has no telegraph as yet, so the message about Donald just got through to me about a week ago. I came out as soon as I could.'

'Where from?'

'I live near Yuma, working as a hostess in one of the saloons there – the Border Bar – don't look at me like that, I know what hostess means in most of those places, but its not like that, they've been good to me.'

'What about your family?'

'Them? Let's just say I had to get away from them. Dad's a bully even though he thinks he knows what to do all the time, and they're dirt poor. I just wanted to see a bit of life, so I set out to travel the territory, had a few men-related encounters I'd rather not tell you about, and ended up at the borders. Once I get enough money I'm off again. At least if this blows over.'

'So you came to the farm and you've been here since?'

'No,' she took a deep breath and it was evident to him that she wanted to unburden to him. 'I got to the farm and found it was abandoned. I looked everywhere for them then I went into town where I visited the obvious person – that lawyer, Spendlow. Agnes told me in one of her letters he had been dealing with them in some way. He gives me the shudders.'

'Really? He seemed all right to me.'

'You're not young and female. The whole time I was there he seemed to be undressing me with his gaze. I liked his clerk, Spangles, but Spendlow is a creep. Anyway, when he told me that my sister had gone back to the family I just didn't believe him, and I have no way of telling. But that was when he told me the worst news that she could not have known.'

'What was that?'

'When Donald died, the land, which was in his name only, did not automatically pass to my sister. In less than two days the thirty days are up and the land reverts to the town.'

'But you could have acted on her behalf, putting in a claim.'

'That's the problem,' she said, 'they only allow a certain amount of claims – and they've already been made.'

'Then, if you don't mind me saying so, I don't see why you're here.'

'Because it's a cheat, crooked, evil and downright wrong, that's why,' said the girl.

'I can see why that would make you stay and defy them – whoever they are.'

The conversation would have continued but there was a slight distraction that turned into a major one. A lithe dark-haired figure leapt out of the trees near the house, the girl was still holding her gun, and she was about to raise the weapon when it was knocked out of her hand by the man to whom she had been speaking so calmly just a second before. In the meantime the new arrival covered a large amount of ground in a surprisingly short time, seized hold of her and held a wicked-looking knife to her throat. She was dressed in black, baggy trousers, and wore a heavy cord jacket over her more feminine blouse. This, and the fact that she was wearing a wide-brimmed hat would have fooled a casual observer into thinking she was of the opposite sex.

'Firebrand,' said Thorne, 'remember your manners, let go of the lady right now!'

Brand pulled back and saw that he was indeed facing a young woman – not a bad looking one either. He had the grace to look slightly ashamed of what he had done, but not for long, because the gun was still lying on the ground in front of her and she was not about to surrender easily to what she now thought were her enemies.

Annie dived forward and scooped up the weapon, but as she stood there with it in her hand she found that Thorne was pointing his Peacemaker straight at her.

'Annie, I don't want to do this, believe me, but someone is going to get hurt with that thing. Do us both a favour and drop it.' A look of terrible defiance written on her pretty face, she did as she was asked. 'Brand, pick it up.' The half-breed obeyed.

'You won't get away with it, you murderers,' she said.

'Really? I'm just trying to stop any of us being hurt,' said Thorne. 'Get in there and we'll get a coffee, it's thirsty work searching about an old place like this.'

'Then you're really not here to enforce an order?' She gaped at him.

'I think we established that before,' said Thorne.

'When I heard gun shoot I was over at edge of field,' said Brand, 'tripped over in haste to get back. I thought something had happened to boss here.' It was the nearest he could come to an apology.

The girl looked from one face to another. Neither of the men was smiling at her; they were too concerned about what she would do next, and then she gave a deep sigh.

'Let's go in and see what we can do.'

Luckily there was water in a well in the yard – Jubal knew that if you dug deep enough anywhere around here you would find a reasonable supply of water because much of the monsoon rain soaked into the ground and ran along hidden, rocky canyons. He fetched a bucketful from the well and prepared a fire inside the living area that also served as a kitchen. The store cupboard was not exactly full.

'It's not real coffee,' he grunted, 'smells like chicory, but it'll have to do, if that's OK with you ma'am?'

'It will, and me being used to best china tea and cakes,' she said.

It was the drinking together of something that resembled a beverage that seemed to persuade her that the man with the partially ruined face was on the side of the angels. They sat around the table to have a talk. Thorne watched her behaviour with Brand, but she seemed to accept him immediately, which made her the kind of person he would want to help.

'My advice,' said Thorne, 'would be to go into town and find some kind of lodgings and a job, until all of this blows over. In the meantime you can try and find out if your suspicions about what has happened to your sister are true.'

'I don't think so,' the girl tilted her chin in an eerily familiar way and for a second he was taken back to his conversation with her sister.

'So what exactly are you intending to do?'

'I'm going to stay right here and defend what belongs to me by right until my sister returns or we find out what happened to her. I'm not for shifting.'

'I hope you realize that next time it won't be somebody who is here out of personal concern. It will be whoever the authorities back in town decide is going to represent them – and they'll be prepared to use a great deal of force.'

'Next time I won't make myself visible, I've learned my lesson with you. Remember I've never done anything like this before.'

'And I can't get you to leave here for your own good?'

'No.'

'Well, the danger point seems to be the next two days. If you're gonna stay here I guess I better get you sorted out. How did you get here?'

'I have horse, a sorrel, he's out in the old barn.'

'Right, well I suggest you hide him somewhere amongst the trees. The weather's not too bad, so we'll get you a bedroll, a tent and make sure you can rest somewhere overnight. During the day we'll have a patrol. This ain't that big a property.'

'You've done this kind of thing before,' she said in a tone that was half-admiring and half questioning.

'Yep, and succeeded too. There's another principle of legality here that the lecherous lawyer failed to point out to you, and that's the fact that possession is nine points of the law around here. You're doing the right thing.'

'Young woman, she isn't safe,' said Brand, but with a faint gleam in his eye that said he was not indifferent to her looks.

'Never mind the star-gazing,' said Thorne, 'I want you to get the buckboard, go into town and get me a list of things she'll need. A couple of gold eagles'll pay for the lot.'

'I will go,' said Brand. Thorne began to reach inside his jacket where he kept his coins in a pouch. The girl flushed with annoyance.

'I'll pay!'

'No you won't,' said Thorne, 'I'm guessing you don't earn much, that you spent a great deal of your savings on that gun. Don't worry, though, I'm not insulting you. You can pay me back with whatever you earn when all this is over.' He gave a firm nod, Annie subsided and Brand left on his errand with a list of items.

CHAPTER SEVEN

Brand rode a brown mare called Wild, an example of his sense of humour because she was one of the most placid creatures he had ever owned. He would have preferred his stallion, Ghost, but that particular animal was somewhat reactive, not good to take on a mission where neither of them knew what they were going to encounter. He went back to Thornelea – as Frank's former spread was called – and harnessed Wild and another horse to the buckboard and set off into town.

As he rode into town, Brand thought deeply about the situation he was going into with 'boss man', as he liked to call his friend Jubal. He knew, as many did not, what it was like to stand up to any kind of declared authority. He decided to stock up well on the things that they would need to help the woman, Annie, prepare for a siege at her sister's farm including food items, a tent and blankets.

The town was busy as he rode in. This was a prosperous place, made so by the mines, the cattle trail, and the lavish spending of Jackson Earl. As he predicted, when some of the townspeople saw him dismounting in Main Street he was greeted by many hostile looks. One or two women even gathered their children to them and marched off in the opposite direction. Memories were long in this part of the world, especially when Apache raids were still happening in other parts of the territory.

The general store had a facade that curved up and above the actual building, proclaiming what it was in big letters stencilled in red. The store owner, a paunchy man called Danvers on the wrong side of sixty, came forward as the Indian entered.

'What do you want boy?'

Brand immediately knew what to do. If he showed any great intelligence he would be treated badly and might not even get the goods he was sent for.

'Boss Thorne, he send me with marks-on-paper,' said Brand, handing over the list he himself had written on the back of an old envelope found at the Greene home. He did not, of course, point out that he was the writer.

'Must have rocks in his head giving an Injun his cash,' said the owner. 'All right, I'll get these things; you just wait here and don't touch anything.' He shuffled off. Brand knew better than to try and help, Danvers knew exactly where everything was and would have resented an intruder pawing at his goods.

Finally Danvers piled the goods – including blankets, pillows, various items of hardware and some food in jars and cans on top of the counter.

'Stocking up eh?' said Danvers. 'Show me your money boy.' Brand handed over the gold coins and the store owner gave them a thoughtful bite before accepting each one. 'All right, fine, now be off with you boy, I've other customers to deal with.' It was late afternoon and the shop was empty, but Brand knew exactly what was being said. *We don't want your type hanging around too long.*

He took the goods outside, taking a couple of trips to do so and put them on the buckboard. He then put a canvas cover on top, securing the whole thing with a piece of rope. He was not the least bit bothered by the stares of people who continued to pass by. News of who was or was not in town travelled fast. The first time he knew he was in some kind of trouble was when he saw four men approaching and recognized Lannigan right away. He had seen their horses tied up in front of the saloon earlier on and had thought nothing of it.

Brand was within seconds of getting out of there. He made his way along the boardwalk. The air was dusty from passing traffic and he could taste the spicy sand at the back of his throat. He just wanted to get back to Annie's ranch. A large man blocked his progress. It was Bug himself. Brand could smell the raw spirit on his breath. It seemed he had been enriching the Gold Rush by gulping down a good amount of the local rotgut.

'Well, looks as if we got us a little friend from the farm,' said Bug with ugly humour. 'You been buying for your boss?'

'Yes.' Brand backed away and nearly found himself in the arms of Pine, who had sneaked up behind him. Pine was not as big as Lannigan, but he had a wiry look about him as befitted an ex-miner.

'Looky see,' said Pine, 'this 'un nearly bowled me over Bug, bad manners that wouldn't you say?'

'Sure is,' said Bug.

Brand did not say anything. He tore away from them both, skipped around Lannigan and out on to the road. Perhaps he could get into the driving seat from there. This time he ran straight into the arms of Clarke and Binns, who had been waiting for him. They pushed him back towards Bug.

His temper rising, Brand thought of the razor-sharp knife in his boot.

*

Jubal Thorne did not waste much time when he was left alone with Annie. He sensed that she still did not trust him one hundred per cent, and he thought she was quite right. If their positions had been reversed he would have been suspicious of her motives. After all, what reason would a stranger have to help somebody he had never met before, especially when there might be violence involved at some point? As they walked around the farm looking for a suitable place for her to shelter the thought nagged at his mind.

'I've changed my mind about leaving you here. Help us both, come into town with me and we will soon be able to sort this out. I'll back you up. Sometimes you're better confronting a problem head on, Annie.'

'What do you mean, come into the town? I have been there. I did not like what I found there.'

'No, me neither.' He studied the spot where she was going to shelter. 'This isn't the only thing you need to do. You're just waiting for trouble here. In my experience waiting for trouble is not a real good thing. You're far better marching into town and facing those who said that you didn't have a claim. I'll back you up because us farmers have to stick together.'

'When I came here I thought I was going to be looking after my sister and the little ones. If I leave here I'm not doing that.'

He could have argued with her further, but he could see that if he continued his argument she would turn against him and ask him to leave, and he did not want her to face her future problems on her own. She was standing on his ruined side and could not read the emotions on the mobile part of his features, and for that he was grateful.

'All right, if you're that determined we'll stay, but Spendlow is just another businessman you know, if you could buy some time by seeing him that would be to your advantage, that's all.'

There was a great deal more going on than helping a stranger. For a start she was a member of a family he had known and liked, and even though he had never met Annie in his life before she was the image of her sister, and needed protection. Part of him though, knew that this wasn't the only reason he was coming to her aid. That part of him knew that he had been a farmer for long enough, that this was the real Thorne shining through the rural veneer.

At last they found a clump of cottonwood trees that grew reasonably close to the farmhouse but far enough for her to shelter away from a possible attack. If it rained, which was unlikely at this time of the year, she would be protected by the leaves and still able to remain reasonably warm and secure. She would even have a tent and branches to form a minor lean-to if things got rough.

'When Brand comes back you'll have dried beef jerky and cooked beans in glass jars, along with some sweets. It won't be a lot to live on, but if this blows over as quickly as I guess, it will be enough to do you.'

'Thank you Mr Thorne, I really will repay you for all your help.'

'The name's Jubal, your word is good enough for me Miss Annie. You are real determined to stay, but if what I hear is true they wouldn't hesitate to murder you. And you're a looker, if you don't mind me saying so, and they just might attack and violate you first. It's a shocker to say that, but it's true and that's a warning. Tell me, is there a possibility that your sister would have done what they said and just abandoned this place for good?'

They were standing beside the trees now and looking across at the mean little building. Annie squinted at the place that had once held the hopes and fears of her widowed sister.

'You know what? I guess there's every chance that she would have done precisely that thing. But then from what I've heard she wasn't in her right mind after the death of Donald. Even if she did leave of her own accord, that's no reason why some authority should come in and take away what the two of them built up over the last ten years.'

'Well put. But I wouldn't underestimate what you're up against.' He looked at the sky and frowned.

'What's wrong?'

'Judging by the position of the sun, Brand should have been back at least half an hour ago.'

'Well, I'll just check for whatever else I can find to make me more comfortable out here.'

'You do that.' He headed towards the side of the barn where he had tied up his horse.

'Where are you going?'

'To get him back.'

CHAPTER EIGHT

Thorne got on his mount and rode off without a backward glance now that he was sure she would keep safe and avoid any foolhardy confrontations. That the confrontation would come, he had no doubt, but he wanted to be there when it happened.

He was more worried about Brand than he cared to admit. People had unjustified hostility towards those they saw as different.

As he pulled around the corner into Main Street he knew that he could not have been more correct. Brand was there all right. He was in the midst of a group of four men, all of whom were openly taunting the Indian, and it was obvious from a cut beneath his eye, that Brand had already taken some rough handling from the four. Thorne did not hesitate; throwing off his horse, he landed square beside Binns and threw the man to ground so swiftly, and with such a jarring force that Binns lay there quite winded. This created a gap and Thorne jerked his head at Brand as the other three men stared at him, too astonished to react.

'Get on the buckboard. Get outta here now.' The Indian scrambled to obey, but as he passed Thorne he gave a questioning look.

'No, keep out of it, just get going. I can handle this.'

Brand scrambled on to the driving seat, but did not immediately crack the reins. He looked back and saw that Lannigan was staring straight at him. A look of pure fury on his face, Brand took his sharp knife from the side of his boot – during his torment it was on the verge of being used – he lifted the blade as he stared into Lannigan's eyes with his own liquid glare and drew the knife symbolically above and across his throat. Replacing the weapon he gave a high yikking noise and cracked the reins. The horses bolted along the road, the buckboard rattling behind them so that the whole ensemble was soon lost in a cloud of dust. Brand would have preferred to stay, but he had dealt with that stern look before and he wasn't about to defy his friend. Binns scrambled to his feet and swayed from side to side as he recovered from his fall. Pine and Clarke moved in on the newcomer.

'Wait,' said Thorne. He was such a commanding presence that the two men hesitated, with Clarke, a smaller man looking over his shoulder at Lannigan for reassurance. Tormenting Brand was all very well, but Thorne was a prosperous landowner. Lannigan, big man that he was, held still as if he was mulling over the situation before taking any kind of action.

Thorne did not pay any attention to those he regarded as lesser mortals. He was after the big prize, knowing instinctively that if he could face up to Bug he would win the battle. He had confronted many enemies in his time, some of them instinctive tormentors like Bug and in many cases by sheer force of personality he was able to get them to back down. He didn't think that would happen in this case because Lannigan was one of those rare combinations; he was a bully who struck out hard when he was defied. Besides, he was here with his men. In a one-to-one confrontation there was every chance that he would think better of his behaviour and slink off, but not here where he would lose face.

'What's going on here?' demanded Thorne as he looked straight into the piggy eyes of the chief tormentor. 'You're delaying my business and that ain't good in my line of work.'

'Hell,' said Bug, 'we was just having a little fun with yore employee, that the truth boys?' At these words the three other men gave a mutter of agreement. Binns had a hand on the butt of his gun, but had not yet drawn the weapon and started forward because all four of them were now facing the new arrival.

'Let me get him, boss.'

'Step back,' ordered Lannigan, 'Get easy. After all, Mr Thorne here, he don't know how to take a little joke.'

'The humour of your little "joke" escapes me,' said Thorne. 'But you better keep out of my business and leave my men alone in future.'

'You saw him,' said Bug, 'threatened to cut my throat. Real peaceable that was. Why we oughter go over to the Thorne place and have us a little necktie party just fer that alone.'

'You started it,' said Thorne. 'I saw what you did, and I know why the man behaved as he did.' He knew now that he was getting to the dangerous part of this encounter; what happened in the next few minutes would determine whether he was going to walk away or not.

The cooler air did not help. Some people thought that noon was a dangerous part of the day. This was not the case – although tempers could run high as the heat rose, it was usually too warm for most would-be combatants. When the heat soared through the air they would rather be in the cool of a saloon knocking back some beer to wet

60

their dry throats.

No, Thorne knew that this argument would never have happened in the earlier heat, just as he knew that the cooling air, the half-empty street, would now allow them the space for such a quarrel.

Just as he knew the four of them would defeat him, he also knew it was time for him to make his mark. 'So,' he said in a conversational tone, 'what's it like to be a coward, Bug?'

Although Brand had done as he was asked, he was not the kind of person to abandon the one person who had given him some kind of shelter from a brutal world. The problem was that his employer had made it very clear that the goods were to be taken away, along with his friend. How to square the circle? He would have to defy his orders for the sake of his boss.

The answer was simplicity itself. Brand halted the buckboard in front of the weathered building, where the livery keeper was already outside smoking a cigarette. He wasn't allowed to smoke inside because the building was not only dry, it was filled with straw and a fire would destroy his livelihood. He was a small, quick man called Samms, who didn't mind who his customers were as long as he got paid.

'Look after horses, and cart please,' said Brand, jumping off the seat as he spoke. He took out some of Thorne's money and gave the man an upfront payment.

'Surely will,' said Samms.

'Bonus for you when I come back,' said Brand. He stood for a moment and took his bearings. Behind this part of Main Street were the miner's quarters. If he went that way and along the back of the buildings and along an alley on the far side of the saloon, he would come out roughly where Thorne was. He gave the old-timer a quick salute, and then ran down the side of the livery and past the corral at the back. As he had surmised, this led him to a minor maze of streets that comprised the miners' quarters. He took off to the left and began to travel quickly and silently past the back of the buildings that comprised Main Street. He passed the Celestial Hope Chinese laundry where a large number of garments hung out the back, some of them surprisingly frilly, then the rear of the bank, which was heavily fortified with brick walls and barbed wire at the back, the lawyer's office and finally the saloon. He came to the alleyway at the side of the saloon. He ran along this without thinking, knowing that time was running out. Halfway along, to keep it free from drunks, it was blocked by an adobe wall at least eight feet high.

When told that he was a coward, Lannigan lost all bluster and began to reach for his gun.

'Wait, I'll give you a fair fight, just the two of us, man against man, forget weapons, take off your gun belt, I'll take off mine. We'll go at it. How does that suit you, or are you too afraid of one man?' By now a crowd of curious spectators had gathered. Now, if he shot Thorne along with the help of his men it would be cold-blooded murder in front of a host of witnesses.

'Well?' Thorne gazed at Lannigan, who could not back down or he would lose face in front of his men and the gathering townspeople.

The answer was a strangled curse as the ringleader threw down his hat and unbuckled his gunbelt, which he placed on the boardwalk beside him. Thorne followed suit, but he took off not just his hat, but the long black coat he always wore, dusty at the hem, and threw it down beside the his own gun belt and hat. Without his coat the former bounty hunter was thin, but sinewy, with an air of strength that belied his physical presence.

Lannigan looked at that spare body and grinned at his followers. This would all be over in seconds once he unleashed a few blows on his hapless opponent. In fact, his manner seemed to suggest, he was almost wasting his time – it would take one pounding jar on the chin and Thorne would blow away like tumbleweed.

The situation changed quickly when Thorne swept aside his long coppery hair and tucked it into his collar to get it out of the way. His damaged face and one eye were suddenly and starkly brought into focus. Now it seemed that Lannigan was about to destroy a one-eyed man. But Jubal was not yet finished. He lifted the eye-patch that covered the orb on the left-hand side and exposed not an empty eye socket, as many in the gathering crowd would have expected, but an actual eye.

What an eye this was! The eyeball was exposed where the skin had puckered and fallen away in whatever horrendous fire had caused the damage. With the eyepatch hidden in the fringe of hair that still covered his pale brow, Jubal Thorne's features on that side took on the aspect of a grinning skeleton.

So strong was the impression in the pale light of afternoon that a gasp went up from the crowd. His grinning opponent abruptly lost his smile as he too regarded the figure before him with a sort of superstitious dread.

'There ain't much to you,' said Lannigan, recovering some of his aplomb as he held up his meaty fists. 'Just apologize real good and I'll let you go.' The answer to this was physical. Jubal Thorne came forward moving on his toes so fast that he was almost a blur, and punched Lannigan on the body not just once, but three or four times in quick succession. His big opponent looked down, and then gave a roar of laughter.

'Hardly felt that, if it's all you got. You asked for it!' It was his turn to take a shot at the man who was standing there, bony fists protecting his lean body. Onlookers who expected Lannigan to lumber forward like an ox were surprised when the big man turned out to be unexpectedly light on his feet. It seemed as if the fight would be over in seconds.

There was just one problem with this optimistic forecast. When Lannigan punched out with a fist that should have connected with the face of his opponent his blow met only empty air. The attempted punch had unbalanced the big man so that he had to pull back to stop from falling headlong into the dust. He looked faintly ridiculous and the audience gave a collective, appreciative laugh. When Bug looked around Thorne was standing just out of range glaring at him with that skeletal expression.

Lannigan shook his head as if to clear out a fog from his brain. It was a mistake, that was all; a man was entitled to make a mistake. This time Lannigan was more scientific in his approach, waiting until his opponent showed a gap in his defence.

'Still there?' asked Thorne sarcastically.

Lannigan gave a roar and ran forward, punching out in a manner that would have floored any ordinary opponent. Again his fist met empty air, but this time he was aware of a blow to his ribs that actually hurt. From being a kind of joke that would prove his ability to admit a crushing defeat, Lannigan found that he was in a real match of wits. He smacked out at random and his ill-timed blow connected with Thorne, who fell to the ground. He got to his feet, apparently dazed. It seemed the fight was nearly over.

In the alleyway Brand looked at the high wall and knew that he had no realistic chance of springing to the top.

Fortunately for him this was an alley beside a busy saloon, and at the entrance to the narrow passage were some empty wooden beer barrels, four in all, that had been left at the back of the saloon. He tipped one of the larger barrels on its side and rolled it to the wall. It was an awkward shape but much easier to handle than it would have been if it had been full. He put the barrel upright again, jumped on top, then reached up and hauled his lithe body to the top of the wall.

He had an idea in his head that he would run across from the Gold Rush, punch out the nearest men and drag Thorne away from the fray. In his own mind he saw this as some noble act of rescue. Then they would run to their transport and make their way out of town.

He was sitting atop the gritty brickwork when his eyes were caught by the swelling crowd and the second act of the fight, but he stayed his hand when he saw what was happening across the wide, dusty street.

Now that he had his chance, the bigger man lunged forward to finish the fight and leave his crushed opponent on the ground. This was a big mistake because Thorne had only been pretending that he was dazed. As the big man came closer and threw his punch, Thorne said a few words that infuriated his opponent even more.

'Is that all you've got?' He dodged down rather than aside and treated his opponent to a flurry of blows to the ribs that would have had little effect singly, but had the cumulative effect of tenderizing though not actually breaking some of his opponents' ribs.

The crowd who had gathered at the first intimation of a fight, drawn out of workplaces and saloons, gave an appreciative roar when they saw Thorne doing this. This, they felt, was the work of a master.

With Lannigan, his stubborn nature, and the fact that he was now being watched by about seventy of his contemporaries, drove him to continue with a course of action that was downright foolhardy in the face of the other man's tactics.

'I'll get you, you little bastard,' he roared, holding up his fists again, rushing forward and punching out at that grinning face Thorne was no longer there. But as he moved lightly away he swung out and smashed Lannigan right on the nose, which promptly began to bleed at a level that made it look like a minor tributary of the Colorado.

The blow on the nose had sapped all of the bigger man's will to go on. He jumped forward again and made another half-hearted smash at Thorne's infuriating grin, and once more received a flurry of blows to the ribs that made them even more tender and sore to the touch.

Binns, who had his own reasons for disliking Thorne, mainly to do with being winded earlier, began to draw his Smith & Wesson from its holster. He was stopped by the firm hand of Pine.

'Don't be stupid, there are about a hundred witnesses here. Do that and you'll be swinging from the wooden arm outside the sheriff's office by nightfall.'

Having a healthy sense of self-preservation, Binns saw the sense in this and relaxed his gun arm.

'Speaking of the sheriff,' said Clarke, 'look what's going on.' Sheriff Bradley rode up with his two deputies, dismounted and began to make their way through the gathering.

Everyone liked a good fight; there was no doubt about that. The problem was that it led to disruption in public order, shootings and more shootings then possible revenge attacks that could go on for years on end. Morton

Bradley had seen such things happen before, so it was in everyone's interests to break them up before they became too serious. The trouble was, as soon as he went amongst the spectators he was hemmed in by the good citizens of Earlstown.

There was a figure emerging from the house on the hill, a formidable man, who even at a distance seemed to be better clothed and fed than many of the town's inhabitants. This was Jackson Earl.

He had been alerted to the fight by the noise of the crowd a few minutes earlier. At first he had thought nothing of it. Fights were common in town, mostly between drunks who had started their quarrel in the saloon only to have it carry over into the street. This one was unusual because it was early in the evening. When he came out and looked more closely, though, noticing even at a distance who was actually engaged in battle, his whole attitude changed at once and he went for his horse, riding down on his own account.

As for the fight, it was in the very last stages. Lannigan gave up all pretence of fisticuffs and lunged forward with a roar that seemed to shake the very ground, arms open, ready to grab his opponent and crush him against that bear-like body.

In this case success did not occur because Thorne once more danced to one side, but this time he smashed Lannigan on the side of the head, danced around him again and smashed him on the other side of the head.

The blows had the effect of dizzying the big man. A sea of faces swam before him, with that grinning face in the middle, and then he fell to the dust.

The fight was over. The crowd gave a series of resounding cheers.

Thorne quietly began to gather his worldly goods

including his hat, his coat, and his gun belt. It was obvious that he was finished. The sheriff had halted with his deputies in the middle of the crowd. It was obvious that he was going to let this one go.

Dizzy though he was, Lannigan rolled over towards the boardwalk, snatched at his own gun belt that still lay there. He was unable to stand, but his coarse features were contorted in fury as he snatched out his pistol and aimed at Thorne's back while that person was putting on his coat. There was a warning shout from the remaining spectators, because the crowd had started to drift away as soon as they saw the fight was over, and Thorne began to turn, but it was obvious that he would be too late and would get killed by a man who no longer cared but just wanted revenge.

CHAPTER NINE

Lannigan felt a sharp pain through his wrist as a quirt slashed at his forelimb. He gave a cry of pain and dropped his weapon to the ground as all the strength went out of his arm.

Jackson Earl was standing over him with a look of fury on his face. This was the true man. He was better fed and better clothed than most of the townspeople, but he was showing the man he had been in his early days, the ruthless mine owner who was not going to countenance this kind of trouble in his own town.

'You,' he said to the three thugs, referring to Lannigan, 'help him up and get him the hell out of here. If I see his face again today I won't speak for what will happen to any of you. A fine job you're doing Mort.' He turned his attention to the sheriff as the three subdued thugs helped their leader to his feet. Lannigan had to be supported on either side by two of them and was hastily trailed off.

'I thought it was just an ordinary street brawl at first,' protested the sheriff, turning to Thorne. 'I guess I'll have to arrest Bug for attacking you, mister.' There was a faint plea in his voice. The former bounty hunter looked more like his old self with coat and hat on, and his eye patch restored. His coppery hair partially concealed the ruined

69

side of his face.

'I ain't about to press charges, too much bother. I guess he's learned his lesson, I don't want to start some sort of feud.' The sheriff looked relieved at this news.

'That's exactly what I was hoping we could prevent.'

'Thanks sheriff,' the two men looked at each other with a little more respect. Bradley departed with his deputies.

'Guess we can talk business,' said Jackson Earl, who had kept silent during this exchange.

'In what way?' asked Thorne in return.

'Mr Thorne, your brother Frank was a good man. A lot of heart went out of him when he lost Belle. He didn't just lose a wife – he lost a son. He just closed his doors and became a recluse, and the place went to the dogs as they say.'

'I think I know what you're driving at.'

'Sometimes a man has got know when to fold his cards and steal away from the table. It's no secret around here that I like a bet with the best of them.' This was true; from gossip he had picked up in town Thorne knew that over the years Earl had won – and lost – prodigious sums of money at the card table. 'I'm betting, Thorne, that you took on that farm out of a sense of duty, maybe felt an obligation towards your brother. Well you discharged that obligation a long time ago. You ain't a farmer, it's not in your blood, but I saw the way you handled Lannigan. You're a fighter, always have been, always will be.'

'Cut to the chase.'

'I'll make you an offer for the land, a fair one. You sell and get out of here for good. Your brother's dead, no amount of back breaking work will restore his life.'

'Earl, I'll think about it,' said Thorne.

'That's good enough for me, see me soon.' Earl strode off to his horse at the same second as a buckboard driven by a young Indian rumbled down the road. He had done the sensible thing by going back for the carriage when the fight was won.

'Need a ride?' asked Brand coming to a halt beside his boss.

'Let's get back to Annie,' said Thorne, 'She must think we've abandoned her.' He sat in the driving seat and took over the reins. It wasn't long before they were heading out of town. Thorne ached all over from the fight with Lannigan; the ill-paired boxing match had taken more out of his spare frame than he might have cared to admit. He was hot, too, from his exertions and had thrown his coat into the back of their carriage.

'I was trying to get to you, got in back of saloon, saw you fighting,' said Brand. 'So ran back to get buckboard. Knew you were doing pretty well. Especially when rest couldn't lay a finger on you. What with the sheriff there.' He did not say so, but the fight had impressed him more than anything else he had ever seen his friend do.

Between them was the unspoken agreement that it was time to get out of town for the simple reason that Lannigan might be crushed right now, but his three men were still around and might decide it was time to kill the two as they saw it 'trouble makers' and to hell with the consequences.

Because he was concentrating so much on getting back to Annie, Thorne let his guard drop with terrible consequences.

The road out of town was not entirely straight, with rocky outcrops on either side. As they passed one of these areas on the way back to the farm a loud shot rang out, followed by another. Luckily they were going forward at a great pace or the consequences might have been a lot worse. Thorne gave a loud groan of pain and dropped the reins from his hands as the punch of the bullet that hit him knocked him to one side. Luckily the second had missed completely. They began to slow down.

'Take the reins,' commanded Thorne, 'get us out of here.' Brand did as he was ordered while Thorne withdrew his gun despite the pain shooting through his body and fired into the area where the shots had come from at random. He knew that the gunman, whoever it was, would be in fear of a stray bullet and would lie low; this would buy them the time to get the hell out of there. The buckboard moved fast. Thorne did not say anything, but he clutched at his left shoulder and red liquid began to seep though the cloth of his striped shirt.

By the time they arrived at Annie's farm, Thorne had his eyes closed and it seemed that he was just managing to keep from fainting from the pain. The light of day was already fading as the carriage rumbled into the yard. Annie came forward from where she had been hiding.

'Where the heck were you?' she demanded, stopping all enquiries when she saw what had happened to Thorne. Together they assisted him to get down from his seat.

'Get me in, see how bad it is,' grunted Thorne to the girl. 'Brand, you take the buckboard, house it, unload the goods and hide the horses. Get me into the farmhouse,' he said to the girl.

'What if the attack comes?'

'I don't think we'll be seeing anyone tonight.' She did not argue any further, but led him into the building where she got him to sit down while she eased the coat off his shoulders. She gave a low exclamation when she saw the wound.

'Looks as if the bullet went clean through you.' She did not hang around, but found some cotton and linen, cleaned the wound and bound it up.

'Glad it went through,' grunted Thorne. 'That means it shouldn't fester.' He gave an involuntary groan as he stood up.

'Where are you going?'

'To give Brand a hand, we've got to get you set up.'

'You're not going anywhere. You look exhausted. You say you don't think they're going to be here tonight?'

'We'll still keep watch.'

'Maybe so, but you're going to sleep in my sister's room. I'll get set up, and then take turns with your man at keeping watch.'

'Well I think we made the right choice in helping you,' said Thorne admiringly. 'I won't say this is a scratch, but it ain't the worst wound I've ever had.'

'It's me,' said Brand before coming in. 'It's all set up way you wanted,' he added. 'You can shelter there at once,' he told Annie.

'I can't persuade this man to rest,' she said.

'Boss, we'll be all right, I can't see anyone attack us tonight.'

'All right, I'll agree to rest in here with a lit candle, staying armed.' They agreed to this because it was obvious that he was not going to go into the back room. They solved the problem by dragging through the cot bed that had once contained the two children, and putting the other mattress on top. This raised him up in a satisfactory manner with his back against the wall and a gun at his side on the table. He insisted on these arrangements.

Luckily Annie had also found a bottle of whiskey. This was also useful because Thorne drank some of the whiskey whenever he felt the inevitable waves of pain from his fresh wound.

The pain did not worry him because he knew from past experience that pain could be controlled, had to be subdued for the sake of what he was doing, protecting a young, beautiful woman and her property.

Somehow, as the evening hours ticked past, he managed to sleep.

CHAPTER TEN

The pain in his shoulder woke him the next morning. Annie came in holding a shotgun and lit a candle because it was just getting light outside and the interior of the cottage was extremely dark. She examined the wound in the feeble light.

'It looks clean,' she said, 'hopefully you'll be lucky and it won't fester.'

'Luckily the air around these parts will help,' said Thorne. 'It's clean, and dry when you're away from the sand. Where's Brand? On guard?'

'No, he's away at Thornelea, said that he had to see to the animals and fetch a few more goods.' Thorne merely nodded, knowing that looking after the welfare of the stock and making sure they were taken care of was typical for Brand.

'When did he leave?'

'A couple of hours ago, he's only had about four hours sleep. You've had less, really because I heard you shouting out loud, with the pain, I was going to come in a couple of times but you told me to leave you alone, so I did, seeing as how you had a gun at the side of your bed.'

'To be honest I can't remember much, I was drifting in

and out of dreams all night, some good, some bad. Mostly bad.'

He stood up and tested his left hand. Luckily the bullet did not seem to have done any permanent damage, because he could move all his fingers, but whenever he flexed them he felt rushing pains that were almost too agonizing to bear.

He asked for assistance from Annie – no point in aggravating the wound – and put on his gun belt and then his long, black coat. Standing there in the light that gathered through the window he looked and felt more like his old self. But despite being armed, even if Brand was sensible enough to bring his other gun and spare bullets, he was in effect a one-armed gunfighter. He would have to rely more on his ability to bluff his way through any situation that might arise. He had done this more in his life than he might care to admit.

'Right, let's get outta here,' he said. 'As far as I'm concerned the more we hang around here the more chance they'll get us first go. We need to steal a march on them, not the other way about.'

They went out into the yard and headed towards the fringe of trees over the other side. As they did so, a dark figure stole into view between them and their new shelter. Thorne drew his gun. He felt an ache as he drew the weapon because the action gave him a twinge on his bad side.

It was Brand.

'It wasn't me,' he said, holding his hands up and giving a grin. The gunman and the girl relaxed a little. They went to the makeshift shelter amongst the trees. It was deep enough in that she would be able to hide successfully, but close enough so that she would keep an eye on the building and find out if any intruders had appeared.

Brand had brought some cooked, smoked meat back with him. It was bound up in cloth and would last for a while. He had also brought a stock of bullets and Thorne's other gun.

'What makes you think they'll be here?' asked Annie.

'You have something they want,' replied Thorne simply. Now all they could do was wait.

The watchers had overestimated how early the intruders would be on the road, and it was past eleven before four horsemen came into the yard and hitched their horses beside the barn. They would have been recognized by most people in the district right away because the party consisted of Bug Lannigan and his three men.

'You stand there as the lookout and the rest of us will go have a look-see,' said Lannigan to Binns. Bug headed with the other three towards the low building, where Pine looked at his boss for some kind of hint before kicking in the front door. All of them had their guns in their hands and Lannigan went in first. There was no doubting his courage even if it was greater than his intelligence.

'Well look at this,' he said, standing in front of the makeshift bed. 'Seems she's been carving out a little nest. Time for this bird to be evicted.'

'One of the pillows has blood on it,' said Pine, examining the bed more closely. 'Don't know how that could have happened.'

'Food's been eaten here,' said Bug, as he sniffed the air. 'There's a candle been burning here as well. Let's have a look in the stables and the barn.' He had relaxed and holstered his gun and the other two followed suit.

They went outside, only to find that Binns was standing in front of the farmhouse with a look of sullen resentment on his fleshy features. This would have been strange

77

enough, but facing the other three as they came out were some unwanted figures from the day before. Thorne and Brand stood at a distance of about twelve feet from each other. In between them stood the girl, hatless, the sun on her fair hair reflecting glints of gold. She was nursing a Winchester '73 in a gross parody of motherhood, and moreover she looked as if she could use the weapon. From the expression on her face she was quite prepared to do so. This was one baby that could spit fire.

'I couldn't help it boss,' said Binns. 'They sneaked up behind me and told me to throw down my gun.' The Peacemaker at the back of his head had been a further inducement to do so.

'Shut up,' said Lannigan. 'I'll deal with you later.' Binns came over and joined his friends at a sharp order from Thorne.

'State your reasons for being here and state them clearly,' said Annie in a voice that was firm rather than threatening. She did not look a woman who was going to back down soon.

'Miss Annie, I know you think you're doing the right thing, but this farm ain't yours any more,' said Lannigan. 'Now I'm asking ya to get off this property real peaceful and we'll call it a day.'

'You have no authority to be here,' said Annie. 'This land, this property belongs to my relations and I'm standing in for them when they're not here.'

'Miss, you have to understand, this here land's gone back to the county and there ain't a thing you can do about that. Now we was sent here to get you to go peaceful like or we was to take you off the land.'

'Is that so mister? You ever hear the saying that possession is nine points of the law? This land belongs to me right now until my sister and her children come back and that's all there is to it.'

'You better miss, or the truth is you're breaking law and you'll be arrested for the lawbreaker you are.'

'And who is going to arrest me? You and your bully-boys? Well I don't have a legal background, but it seems to me you've just been told by some higher-up to come and chase me way from what's mine. Looks to me as if you don't represent the law at all. I don't see your badge.'

'I am here with these men on the authority of the town.'

'So what you're telling me is that a town is a living, breathing thing? A town is mostly run by men, and it's a man has told you what to do.'

'I'll ask you again to leave peaceful like, then it's going to be time for action.'

'Well I'm just plain not going. I'll be dead before you get me off this land.'

'That can be arranged,' snarled Binns, who seemed to be taking the whole thing personally. Lannigan swung a meaty fist and landed a blow that almost knocked the man off his feet.

'I said to you, to shut up.' He faced Annie. 'You are a mighty fine looking filly; I wouldn't like to see you get on the wrong side of the law, and you mixing with those two miscreants. You know they caused a whole heap of trouble in town yesterday? That black-coated scarecrow cheated in what shoulda been a fair fight and that heathen Injun threatened to slit the throat of an upright citizen, didn't he boys?' Clarke, Pine and Binns nodded in agreement. 'So the less you associate with them two the better because they'll land you in so much trouble you'll wish you had never come here.'

'So that's all you have to say? I reckon you go off now and don't come back.'

'What if I tell you I ain't going?' Lannigan's hand hovered above his gun and his men followed suit, including Binns who looked down in sudden panic as he realized that he had an empty holster.

'You can draw if you want, but these boys with me will swear I was acting in self defence when I blow your head off,' said the girl. She was so pretty that the words seem to hang there for a moment before Lannigan took in their full import. He gave a snarl of annoyance, snatched at his gun and pulled it level to point at the girl. His men followed suit only to find that they were already at a disadvantage. Three weapons were pointed straight at them, one of them a high-powered rifle that would take any one of their heads off. Lannigan had called their bluff in a gamble that had failed to pay off.

'Bug, I thought from your little encounter with me the other day, you would realize that I am a man who means business. Besides if you're the kind of coward who comes out and shoots at a man from the side of the road I have no regard for you whatsoever,' said Thorne.

'Thorne, the sun has addled your brains,' said Lannigan. 'I don't know about no roadside shootings.' He looked as if he was all set to use his weapon, having reached a point where otherwise he would have to back down. 'I was real busy last night, having a drink with these boys and having a chat with an important man.'

'Well Bug, best to get going and finish your chat.'

It was a going to be a hot day and the sun was sitting in the middle of the sky, but it was not the weather that had caused the beads of sweat to appear on Lannigan's forehead. His hand jerked slightly and there was the roar of a gun being fired, but it was not his weapon that had spoken. His gun spun out of his hand, he gave a shout of pain then cursed loudly and began to wring his hand, the tendons having been painfully stressed when the weapon was torn from his grip.

'Now you boys empty the bullets from your guns,' said Thorne. 'I won't rob you of your weapons since that would give due cause to get the sheriff involved. Brand, give Binns his gun. It's also unloaded by the way.' The other two men obeyed the command to empty their guns, and holstered them while Brand unloaded Lannigan's and handed it back to him, the gang leader snatching at the weapon in an ungracious manner that suggested he might be a little bit piqued.

'Now, thugs, get out of here,' said Annie, stepping aside along with the other two to allow them to get to the side of the barn. Lannigan mounted his horse, wearing a face like granite, and then he turned his mount abruptly, so that Thorne felt as if he was going to use the animal to ride down his enemy.

'This ain't finished,' said Lannigan. 'You and me's got a personal score to settle. Now I'm on business, so I can't do a thing right now, not against the man I'm operating for, but I'll get you soon.' He heeled his animal round, dug in his spurs and followed the rest.

The rest of the day was spent in vigilance, with Brand, Thorne and Annie making sure that the boundaries of the homestead were patrolled on horseback, with everyone remaining armed. Thorne was away for a long time and did not come back until it was dark. Brand too had just arrived from the other direction, where he had been making sure the homestead was still secure.

'What was that you said to Bug about the shooting?' asked Annie when they were having their evening meal.

'Truth is, I wanted to see how he reacted,' said Thorne. 'It looks as if someone wants me six feet under and he seems to have the best credentials for that. But it couldn't have been him shooting at me the other night, or his men, 'cause they didn't pass us and I reckon whoever was out there would need a horse to get that far and try. But it was someone who knew I was on the way out of town.'

'What did you think, then, about his behaviour?'

'He sure is a bully-boy with the backup of his thugs, but I have a feeling that he's not doing this on his own and he's mighty scared of the authorities. I reckon he's on a payroll, that's why he backed down today. A man might do a lot of things for gain but he ain't going to risk death for some paltry pay check that just enables him to gamble a little at faro and get drunk, which is what I reckon he's got.'

'So who is it?'

It was a warm night and they were outdoors, the flickering of their campfire lighting up the little clearing in which they sat. Their food had been cooked on a spit above the fire. The surrounding trees and bushes would stop the glow from being seen from afar.

'You know what? I don't know who's trying to kill me, but I'm going to find out.' There was a chilling note of finality in his voice that sent a tremor along her spine. His voice had been low, soft even, but she wouldn't like to be Thorne's would-be killer when the pair met.

Talking about faro, that very night in the Gold Rush saloon, Lannigan could be found with his companions playing that precise game. He gambled heavily because he was already drunk when he started. He was drunk because he wanted to numb the bad feelings he was getting over his dealings with Jubal Thorne. The saloon was popular with the cowboys who came in mostly at the weekend and it had a few gaming tables devoted entirely to the game. Faro was more popular than poker because it had simpler rules where winning or losing occurred, when the banker turned up cards that were matched by those already exposed. The game had a fast turnover, and it wasn't long before Lannigan lost most of the money he had with him. When he was tired of twisting the tiger's tail, or rather had lost the cash to go on, he staggered to the bar and had one final whiskey before turning to his companions, who were Pine and Clarke. Binns had already said that he was no longer friends with Lannigan, that they were in it only for business from now on.

'So, boys, I'm goin' home to turn in. But before I do, I'm goin' to tell him what I think of him, and the money that he owes me.'

'I wouldn't do that,' said Clarke, who was thin, with hair that was going prematurely grey at the sides. 'He won't like that.'

'We're the ones gettin' in fights and gettin' our hands injured,' said Lannigan, 'but we make pennies.'

'We've done well out of it over the years,' said Pine, who was broader than Clarke but not as mindful. 'We can still do well. It's not the fault of the authorities you spend most of it on booze and cards.'

Lannigan's expression became thoughtful and it was clear that he was considering unleashing some of his considerable physical prowess on his dim-witted associate. He pulled his bulky frame away from the bar.

'I oughter kick ya from here to kingdom come,' he said. 'But I got better plans. 'Less you want to stand me a few whiskies? Or you,' he added to Clarke.

Both men protested that they too were just about cleaned out and Pine had a couple of kids and a wife to look out for, although given the fact he liked to beat her around when he was drunk she didn't really look out for him, except to get out of the way.

'Suit yourself,' said Lannigan. He weaved his way across the crowded saloon with a kind of wounded, drunken dignity. Outside the saloon he walked down past the bank and then into an alleyway that led to the miner's rows where he still lived. A figure stepped out in front of him, barely seen in the dim light from Main Street.

'It's you,' said Lannigan, leaning forward, eyes widening.

These were the last words he ever said as the wicked, slashing blade of the knife cut a gaping wound across his throat and his lifeblood flowed out in a warm, gushing tide. His body pitched forward and he gargled wordlessly for a few seconds, his body twitching in the final throes of death, then he was still.

CHAPTER ELEVEN

Thorne and his companions remained vigilant for an entire day after the visit from the four enforcers from town. Nothing happened in that day, except that the two men were able to make Annie an inventory of stock to be found around the area. There was a lot of work needing to be done to mend fences, and the livestock consisted of a few sheep that ate the low-lying scrub grass in the fields. Some crops needed to be tended. Thorne was not satisfied because he was neglecting his own property and he was worried that if he were away for too long, land-grabbers would come in and try to take the place from him. They wouldn't be allowed to get away with doing so, but he wanted to avoid the necessity of having to fight for his own rights.

'Brand,' he told his friend, 'you go back and check the farm and see how things are going. I'm out to provide a solution for Annie's problems.' He felt they were able to leave her alone because they had worked out a strategy that allowed her to hide from unwanted intruders, and defend her property if need be.

'Will Miss Annie be all right?' asked Brand, the question to Thorne but really directed at the young woman.

'I'll be fine,' she said, 'just make sure you come back later.'

'Will do,' his gaze lingered on her for a moment, a serious look on his young face, and then he was gone.

'What are you going to do?' asked Annie.

'I'm going into town to hire a couple of hands for you, older men who can still help you around here and make sure that everything is kept in order until the return of your sister. Anyway, those old boys being here will give you time to look for her.'

'At least it means I can send a message home. But I don't have much money,' said the girl.

'It's all right, they can help me out at my place too and I'll cover their wages for a few weeks.' The young woman looked at him where they were standing in the yard, with the sun glinting off her fair hair, her full lips slightly parted as she gazed at him, her eyes big and shiny.

'Why are you helping me like this? What are you after, Thorne? A man doesn't do things for a woman for nothing. I'm not going to say I'm an innocent, but I can't repay you that way.'

'You're wrong to think that Annie. You're a good-looking girl and I'm not saying that isn't part of why I'm helping you, but your family have had a terrible wrong done to them, I'm just repaying my debt to your sister.'

Maybe it was his imagination, but a shadow seemed to pass over her pretty face at his words, a fleeting annoyance that he did not desire her in some way. He was not about to tell her the truth, that he looked on her as some kind of wayward daughter; that would annoy her even further. They parted on slightly awkward terms but she did not oppose his plan, knowing that she would at least be able to run the place for a while until she found out what had really happened to the members of her family.

*

As he rode into town, Jubal Thorne considered the matter in hand. His thoughts went straight to Jackson Earl. Of course the thugs were employed by the founder of the town; there was no question that was the case. It was obvious that he used them to do his dirty work. There was no question of that either. The thing to do was to let Earl show his hand more openly. He had nearly done so a few days before when Lannigan had provoked a fight. Like most men who worked behind the scenes, Earl had not been pleased that his puppet had shown him up. Thorne almost laughed aloud at the thought of what he had seen, the expression on Earl's face when he stopped Lannigan from carrying out the act of shooting Thorne, an act that would have put the bully on trial and exposed his master right there and then. Thorne decided that the best thing he could do right now was nothing. He could only hope that the personal antagonism that Lannigan held towards Thorne would not make him launch an attack as soon as he knew the former bounty hunter was in town.

Because Annie's farm was closer to Earlstown, his black horse was soon ambling along Main Street. By then it was past midday and the heat was lying like a blanket on the town. This was good news for him, because he knew where he was heading. He rode past the well-maintained Gold Rush saloon, round the bend in the road, and along to the Skull Bucket, which was a mixture of wood, brick and adobe. It was a low-lying building that had an air of not exactly neglect, with a roof that was made of mud and thatched reeds rather than tiles. It looked like one of the oldest buildings in town. He hitched Spirit to the rail at the side, where the animal was in shade, then walked around the front and into the building.

If the outside was rough and ready, the interior was even more basic. The bar was to the side as you walked through the door, which was an advantage to the barkeep, who could observe whoever was entering and quickly spot troublemakers, of whom there could be quite a few when the cattle riders were in town and looking for a little action.

The bar was as basic as it could have been, consisting of wooden planks held level by uprights so that it was little more than a counter. The surface was far from polished. Behind the bar was a selection of drinks that consisted of the locally brewed sudsy beer, or bottles of rotgut whiskey, tequila, and brandy that had never been within a thousand miles of France. This unvaried selection was doled out by a big man who was slightly curved at the shoulders from having to bend all the time in the lower areas of the saloon. He had a shock of greying hair and his trousers were suspended by braces, worn over a brown shirt that had seen better days.

The furniture was ill-matched and the tables were mostly square with one or two round ones in the mix. The seating was varied, including a few low stools and one or two old tea chests. This was clearly a place where drink was the important factor. As if to prove this, in one of the dark corners at the other side a man sat with a bottle of whiskey beside him and, as Thorne entered, the man poured some into the glass beside him, looked at it like it was some patent medicine he had bought from a snake-oil salesman and swallowed it with great impatience. Other customers sat in pairs, most of them with pipes and cigarettes or foul-smelling cheap cigars.

'You goin' to order mister?' asked the barkeep, getting down to business straight away and Jubal ordered a glass of whiskey. He stood with this in hand as he pretended just to be a local out at noon and just looking for somewhere to get away from the heat of the day.

Looking around, Jubal spotted four men sitting at one of the rough tables beside a tiny window that let some light into the dark interior. All of them had a beer, and they were all playing cards. He saw at once that Tomms, the old man he had met outside the burned-out newspaper offices, was dealing out the cards, and winning too judging from the small pile of coins beside his elbow.

Drink in hand, Jubal sauntered over to where they were sitting, trying to look as unconcerned as possible.

'Joe,' he said, as if talking to an old friend, 'mind if I join you and your friends?'

'Who is it?' asked one of the other men, who had a big, grizzled head, speaking to Tomms rather than Thorne. Tomms hastened to introduce the ex-miners to Thorne. These were Pat Muir, Andy Fine, and Bat McCallum, none of whom were that pleased to be introduced to a man who, by his looks and bearing, was some kind of disturbance to their little world.

'I just came in to have a quiet drink,' he assured them. 'I'm not looking for any kind of trouble. I've met Joe here before, he kind of asked me to look him up some day, so here I am.' He noted the way the other ex-miners looked at their companion with some scorn for having brought this visitor on their heads.

'He ain't got the right,' said Bat McCallum, who was the grizzled looking man. 'That's a fact. We don't want to talk to anybody, especially someone we don't know.'

'I'm a farmer at the head of the valley,' said Jubal mildly. McCallum, who was a man of about sixty, which was old in these parts, stared at him in frank disbelief.

'Andy, Pat, you believe him?'

'Nope,' said the other two almost in unison. Andy was a

89

slight, wiry man, younger than the others but he had something wrong with his right arm. He saw Jubal looking.

'Broke it in the pit in five places, never healed right after that.'

'Sorry to hear about it. Wouldn't stop you doing a few things around the farm though, would it?'

'Mister, me and Pat would kill fer a day's work 'stead of sittin' in this dump. We're barely gettin' by as it is. Pat here has a back problem, hurt it in the mine too. But we can work, and we're willin'.'

Jubal knew it was bad manners to ask how they were managing to get by as it was, but there was probably some mining fund that helped out those who had fallen on hard times due to accidents in the mines. He knew that such events were fairly regular and it was Andy Fine who confirmed what he had already imagined.

'Yep, I was trying to get to a particular seam when the roof came down on me, broke ma back. Took four men to get me out, lucky I wasn't paralysed, and the bones knit over months but I'll never work below ground again.'

'Not many will boys, we all know that,' wheezed Tomms, giving a laugh that turned into a cough. 'Sorry, the old lungs're shot with the dust they garnered down there. Only thing that helps it is beer.' He looked straight at Jubal, who took the hint.

'Four beers,' he said across the room to the barkeep, who began to pour them with that continued look of scorn on his weathered features.

'Tomms, you shut your mouth,' said Bat, who seemed almost frightened despite the fact that he looked the toughest of the four. 'You don't come out with that kind of talk.'

'Well we all like a beer.'

'Stop fooling Joe, you know I'm talking about the

mines. Rest easy with what you say or we could get in more trouble.' Thorne pricked up his ears at this but knew better than to ask too many questions. He could easily lose these men, and that wasn't what he wanted. Again the many years of learning to just wait came in useful. The beers came, he paid for them and there was a noticeable thaw in the atmosphere.

'I want two or more of you to work for Annie Bateman,' he said, 'out on the old Greene farm.'

'I'd do it if it was up to me,' said Bat, he pulled up a crutch that had been lying on the floor beside him. 'This is my spare leg seeing as the other's missin'.'

'I'll do it,' said Pat immediately and Andy nodded in agreement.

'The place is operating under strange circumstances.'

'We know,' said Pat.

'You know?'

'Mister, this is a town where word gets round faster than you can breathe. We know all about Bug and his team and the way they tried to evict the lady. We know she wants to stay put, and if there's coin involved we'll help her out.'

'And what if they come back? Are you willing to stay then?'

'Wages is wages,' put in Andy. ''Sides, Bug ain't a problem any more and I doubt if his sheep'll cause much bother.'

'What do you mean?' Tomms was the one interrupted then. He gave a wheezing cackle that sounded like frightened laughter.

'Mr Thorne, don't you know? Bug Lannigan was found in an alleyway with his throat cut early yesterday morning.'

Thorne seemed taken aback by this news. He knew that the thug was unpopular but this declaration was more than a little unexpected.

'Well nothing I can do about that,' he said. 'Are you two boys up for the work then?' They both nodded their agreement. 'Just general duties. Annie will direct you. I'll help you out with weaponry if you've a mind to have any. You can start this afternoon. There's a bunkhouse on the farm, so you'll have somewhere to stay if you don't want to trail back every night. Just let your grown-up sons and daughters know what you're doing.' He flung a good few silver dollars on the table. 'Take that as a deposit boys, just see that you're there.' As he spoke a ray of light came through the window and caught his face as he stood up, illuminating his ruined features. The men shrank away a little.

'We'll be there,' promised Pat.

'And thanks to you Tomms, you helped me out,' said Thorne, nodding to the old-timer who gave a nod back, the only one who did not seem intimidated by the stranger. Thorne put on his dark hat and began to walk out of the building. The men were already back at their game; they were not going to leave before the heat of the day began to diminish.

Then his eye was caught by the man in the corner. This bookish-looking individual had nearly finished his bottle of rotgut but he was now fixing his hollow-eyed stare on Thorne. This was a challenge that the former bounty hunter could not resist. He went over to the table and sat his battered hat beside the nearly empty bottle.

'You seem to have a problem mister.'

'You should get out of here,' said the drunk man. 'I don't mean this low down hole; I mean this town and this valley. This is no place for a man who wants to tell the truth.'

'Could be,' said Thorne, 'except I feel as if I've been at the blunt end of some home truths for a while.' He had already noted that the man to whom he was speaking had an educated manner and chose all his words carefully. 'Henry Jones?'

'Yes, I am that particular individual.'

'Would you like a drink?'

'No, I would like a bottle.' It seemed a small price to pay for information that might help Thorne survive in the near future. Thorne was desperate to get away from the town and back to his own property, but he was also determined to find out as much as he could. Henry Jones poured a drink from the fresh bottle his companion had ordered. He fixed Jubal with that melancholy gaze.

'I know you, don't I? You are that gunslinger who causes trouble. They call you Blaze because of your coppery hair and the way you use your guns to blaze away at those you attack.' Thorne looked around a little uneasily, but Henry Jones had spoken in such a low voice that his words were lost in the general buzz of conversation from the other tables.

'That's as maybe; I have a new life now. I'm more interested in what you have to say than talking about me. What led up to your office being burned down?'

'Maybe the truth,' said Jones, his melancholy growing even deeper.

'The truth?'

'About the mines.' His voice dropped, he poured another drink and sank it down before continuing. 'Look at them, over there, playing their stupid games. It was Tomms who told me. . . .' His voice tailed off. Jubal felt the growing tide of impatience rising inside him and he bit back a rousing comment. He had a feeling strong remarks would do him no good at all.

'The mines are not doing too well. When certain people came to this area they found gold. That gold ran out after a few years. The silver lode was a lot better, a lot better. Nearly thirty years he got from it. Now it's going the same way.'

'Are you sure?'

'Sure as I can be. Every month they dig deeper and every month they find nothing. They've opened new workings, brought in proper surveyors and done everything they can. Tomms told me because he was scared of the gun-toting individuals led by Lannigan, hired to keep men like him in place. Even the miners who are still working take part in the fiction that more silver will be found eventually because they want to keep their jobs. Most of them should have quit long ago, gone into some other business, but their family, their friends are in this area.'

'But, there was something else.'

'I had to tell the truth, print it for all to see. There was nothing else I could do. *The Town Crier* was my baby, that printing press, I got it brought here in sections, I imported the paper, ink, everything. The truth wasn't good enough, that's why they destroyed me. Never attack the authorities or those who are behind them. I have a big house in the good part of town, but I worked hard with my boys to bring out a decent weekly. Everyone read it, everyone.' The last two words descended into a wordless wail of pain. Ignoring the glass, Henry Jones picked up the bottle and took a long swig of its contents.

'I'm here,' said Thorne grimly, sensing that the interview was over. 'You'll get your newspaper back, I'll make sure that's one of the conditions when this is all over.'

'You – you believe what I'm saying?'

'I don't see why not, you have no excuse for lying. And I'm not about to be scared away from what is mine.'

This time Jones said nothing but his head descended towards his arms and he passed out, head on the table. Thorne suspected from the lack of reaction from anyone in the room that this was not the first time this had happened.

He got up, jammed his hat on his head again and went out into the sunshine, which wrapped around him like a warm blanket. He was not finished with the town yet. He went to the lawyer's office. In a place like this which was not spread out, Spendlow's building stood just a few yards from the undertaker's office. The clerk was in the front office. He was a young man of about seventeen with a presentable bearing and rejoiced in the name of Dickie Spangles. Thorne knew this from previous visits when the former gunman was claiming the rights to his brothers' estate. Like the undertaker's, this building had an inner office that in this case was the sole domain of the lawyer. Thorne liked the lawyer's clerk, with whom he had conversed at length on a previous visit while waiting for the lawyer to become available. The young clerk wanted to know stories about Dodge City and other notorious towns, while he thought that nothing of interest happened in this one. Except for the fight between Lannigan and Thorne which he had seen the other day. Most brawls happened at night when he was back home, and this one had been a doozie.

'I need a word with your employer.'

'Mr Spendlow's a busy man,' said Dickie. 'He's doing a lot of deals right now.'

'Just tell him I'm here.' The clerk disappeared to pass on the information. Thorne looked around at the shabby office and wondered if this was a deliberate ploy to convince people that the lawyer wasn't doing that well. There must be a reason why he was doing a lot of deals, as Dickie had said. The clerk came back.

'He'll see you for five minutes.'

'Thanks.' Thorne strode into the office. His shoulder

was aching and he was tired because his wound was still healing, but he was careful not to let his fatigue show by an expression, word or motion. Spendlow was sitting behind a desk with some large scrolls of rolled-up paper held together with flat green ribbons to one side and some documents in front of him. His expression was not too welcoming.

'Exactly how can I help you, Thorne?'

'You could start by leaving Annie alone.'

'I don't know what you mean.'

'She had a visit from four men who told her, in no uncertain terms, to abandon her sister's farm. She ain't moving, so in the words of the law I would ask you to desist immediately from these activities.'

'Miss Annie isn't under any pressure to leave,' said the lawyer, rubbing the side of his big jaw thoughtfully. 'Even though the thirty days are up, I don't think I would argue against her claim.'

'So you'll leave her alone?' asked Thorne, a little taken aback by this willing agreement to his terms.

'First of all, I have little time to be involved in this sorry affair,' said Spendlow. 'You are jumping to conclusions. Miss Annie Bateman is not under my power, and if a claim is pursued I will give it my attention. As far as I can see she will not be forcibly removed.'

'Well – she'd better not be,' said Thorne, the wind having been taken from his sails. He looked at the rolled up documents, a faint memory stirring of what they represented. 'What's all this?'

'Confidential documents, that is all. I'll have to ask you to leave now. I am a busy man.'

Thorne left the building with dissatisfaction gnawing at his heart. He couldn't make a direct accusation without proof and the one person he needed to see was dead. He did not trust Spendlow when he said that Annie would be left alone. There might be a hiatus of a few days or even weeks, but he knew with certainty that a bid would be made to take her land.

He was tired now, and his shoulder was aching terribly. She had been right about the time it would take him to heal.

The undertaker, Hardin, came out of his door just as Thorne was walking away to fetch Spirit, whom he had hitched across the road at the Skull.

'Good afternoon Mr Thorne, how are you today?'

'I'm fine.' He had rarely felt worse, but he was not about to admit this to an undertaker of all people.

'I trust everything is well with your business?'

'Yep.' Thorne unhitched his black horse, answering shortly because he was not in the mood for meaningless chat. He winced a little as he got on his mount because his sore shoulder was stretched and sent a message of pain like a bolt of fire through his nerve endings.

'You have to watch these injuries. They can turn gangrenous very quickly,' said Hardin. 'I had one client who stepped on a nail one Friday and was dead by the next. We buried him the next day.' Thorne could feel a deep exasperation with the man rising inside him.

'That's interesting information,' he managed to say calmly.

'Perhaps your health would improve if you managed to find a change of scenery,' said the undertaker blandly. 'Well I have to go, a lot of work to do, you know, coffins don't build themselves.' He vanished into the building, leaving behind a man who was not as angry now as astonished. It seemed that when he was dealing with the residents of this town – especially the ones who had some sort of power – he was constantly faced with veiled threats of one kind or another. He was beginning to reassess his analysis of the undertaker, who seemed like a slightly creepy, ultimately harmless man. But like the lawyer, he seemed to have built a wall of words to keep out intruders into the business of Earlstown.

Speaking of the founder, there he was in Main Street having ridden down the hill from his decorative mansion. He had some familiar figures with him; Sheriff Bradley and his two men. The founder was pointing straight at Jubal Thorne in an accusing manner.

'There he is,' said Jackson Earl. 'You men know what to do, arrest him right now!'

CHAPTER TWELVE

The founder of the town did not waste any time, but turned the head of his mount and rode off as rapidly as he had arrived. The sheriff looked grimly at Thorne. Bradley was mounted on a large roan, very much a Mexican style horse, built for stamina with the ability to keep going. His two deputies flanked Thorne on either side while the sheriff had ridden forward and turned his horse across the ex-gunman's path.

'May I ask what this is all about?' asked Thorne mildly. His head was aching now along with his arm and he did not want to provoke some great confrontation. But then again he did not want to be arrested on the whim of some rich man who thought he could order town officials around.

'I think you'll know by now, Thorne. It's the one topic that's been on the lips of every citizen of this town for the past day or so.'

'I was a gunslinger,' said Thorne. 'I'm known in a lot of counties and a dozen states, but I've never murdered a man in an underhand fashion. There's always been a reason for what I've done. Bug was a bully and a fool, but he didn't deserve to be killed like that. And I don't deserve to be arrested on the say so of some rich guy with all the town officials in his pocket.'

'What?' Bradley's skin was already red from the sun, but if possible the colour deepened; this was no blush of shame, it was the redness that comes with anger, 'I ain't in anyone's pocket. See Mr Earl, he's real angry, thinks you should be arrested as a possible accomplice. I'm my own man. I think we'll give you the chance to get the real culprit to come my way. You sure will have to give some evidence, but the real murderer ain't far off of you.'

'I'm guessing you don't mean he's from around these parts,' said Thorne.

'Let the man ride on,' said Bradley conversationally. 'We'll ride along real easy until we get to our destination. Ain't that right Thorne?'

'I guess so.' The sheriff turned his horse and began to ride out of town. Thorne soon came to the sheriff's side with his own animal, which kept up easily with the big roan. The two deputies, young men barely out of their teens rode a short distance behind.

'I guess you owe me a tale,' said Thorne conversationally as they rode along. 'A man doesn't like to be kept in the dark.'

'Sometimes, Jubal Thorne, a feller likes to make his mark for one reason or another,' said Bradley. 'You chose to do that by making sure that Bug Lannigan got his comeuppance in a fight. You know right now you're the most popular man in town for that fight?'

'Am I?' Thorne was genuinely surprised.

'A lot of people disliked him, backed up by his three clowns, thought he was the cock of the walk because he was tight with the boss.'

'And was he?'

'Not up to me to say that, but it sure was a pleasure to see you humiliate that clown. You proved that you were more than a gunman that day – that you could stand up and be counted. Also it was so funny that everyone was busting a gut retelling the tale. Not many's laughing now.'

'So exactly what happened?'

'Mr Earl, he's a big man all right in these parts, but he's an anxious one too. When he can't sleep – which is more often than he'd like – he gets up and patrols the streets of that town behind us.'

'Yes, and what then?'

'He found Lannigan face down on the ground, beside an alley leading to the miners' rows. Lannigan had his throat slit real wide, his head was almost offa his body. Most of his life blood mustta pumped out onto the ground right there and then.'

'I see where this is going.'

'See that heathen of yours? I always say this about half-breeds, it brings out the worst in both races. When he saw how you humiliated the idjit that shoulda been enough, but he has to go and finish the job real good because he thinks he's helping you.'

'Why, even a half-breed is innocent until proven guilty.'

'Could be, except Mr Earl found a black-handled knife mighty like the one your friend announced he was going to use to cut Lannigan's throat. A lotta people won't care much about that old hound dying, but they'll sure care about some renegade Injun taking it on himself to slaughter whites.'

They made rapid progress; Spirit trotted well, even though he was not as fresh as his compatriots, the presence of other horseflesh making him work harder.

The problem was that Brand would actually be at their own homestead today, simply because he would be tending the animals. Theirs was more a crop economy, but the livestock brought in extra money because the pigs and chickens could be bred and sold at the market as well as being a useful supply of fresh meat. Not that they would need much in the way of meat, thought Thorne grimly, thinking of his old ox now freshly smoked and salted down. At least they would have food to supply to Annie until she got on her feet. Thorne did not use his spurs much, but he suddenly pressed them into Spirit, who showed that he could outrace the rest of the animals. This meant that he was a good hundred yards ahead of the sheriff and his men. He gave a sharp, penetrating whistle as he came into the yard. He repeated this three times. This went unheard by the men chasing him because of the sound of three sets of hoofs pounding against the road. Thorne was waiting calmly as they caught up with him.

'You're darn lucky I didn't shoot ya,' said Bradley, 'thought you were making a break for it.'

'Just in case the dogs are out,' he warned the men. 'They tend to launch themselves at new arrivals.' No animals were to be seen. The sheriff and his two men, Bob and Jed, hitched their horses to the main gate and fanned out into the yard, guns in hands as they searched for the accused man. They looked for half an hour but found nothing. Bradley finally came back to Thorne, who had done nothing to either help or obstruct them.

'We know you been helping at Annie's, we're going there, and I hope he surrenders, 'cause if he don't he's a dead man. This ain't our last visit here neither. You should come with us, so we can keep an eye on you.'

'Am I under arrest, Sheriff?'

'No, I guess not,' said Bradley reluctantly. 'The last thing I need to do is bring in a town hero, and personally, after seeing that fight I think you sure had a good reason for keeping Bug alive.'

'Good, because I have work to do.'

They left and Thorne went about his business. His business consisted of going into the main building and collapsing into a deep sleep, troubled only by feverish dreams in which he was being attacked by dark fiends in different shapes and sizes, but whose faces he could not see. Despite being deeply asleep he was instantly alerted when a figure came in through the door of the building and loomed over him. He half-jumped from the wicker chair in which he had been sitting, gun in hand.

'It's only me, boss,' said Brand. 'I hid in hayloft for an hour. It's only matter of time before they come back so had to speak to you.'

'I am going to ask you this once,' said Thorne. 'Did you slit Lannigan's throat from ear to ear and dump his body in an alleyway?'

'Truth is, thought of doing it.' The Indian came in and closed the door. 'But no, I did not kill him. Went on patrol and came back as you asked, rejoined you and Annie. Did not kill him, honest.'

'You were aware he patronized the Gold Rush saloon?'

'Yes. That was across where I stood when he came out with his men to get me. They were trying to make me fight so they could kill me and leave you all alone just like Annie.'

'Lucky you heard my warning whistle.'

'I remember.' One of the ways they had contacted each other out in the wild canyons where a man could get lost in a maze of rock was to whistle to each other. The signals were pre-arranged so that when he had heard the sound of horse hoofs, and a series of whistles meaning that there was some sort of danger around the corner, Brand had dropped everything and had hidden immediately, knowing that he had to do so.

'Looks as if you have to leave now,' said Thorne.

'Because I believe you. I know you're a little hot-headed, but I also believe you're sensible enough to leave well alone.'

'What you mean, "go"?'

'If they see you at all you'll be hanged if they capture you, if you try to escape they'll shoot you dead. Either way you'll be an ex-brave and you're a lot more useful to me alive than you are providing dinner for the vultures.'

'Will not go. You need me to stay.'

'This is blowing over, Brand, Spendlow has already said Annie is not going to be harassed again. I might be a suspect. The best thing you can do is get out of here while you can.'

Brand thought over the matter. He was loyal to Jubal, but also knew that he could cause a lot of trouble for his employer and friend if he stayed.

'Sounds right. I go. Just one thing to say. Supposed to be innocent in eyes of your law, but they think I'm guilty right away. There might be law, but there's no justice.' Thorne found that he was in full agreement with this. It was one of the reasons why he had become a bounty hunter.

'Where will you go?'

'To reservation where white man does not visit now. They will take me back.'

Thorne followed his friend outside and helped equip him for the journey. Brand took his own horse, and the reservation was only ten miles away. They shook hands and Brand was gone, with his former employer watching him leave for just a second before turning in at the road entry to his property.

He did not stay there for long. He had to get back to see Annie and find out if she had managed to meet those who would help her to restore the property. The mere presence of the two men would be reassuring to her. It would mean, with his help, she would be able to concentrate on the more important task of finding out what had happened to her sister. His shoulder was still sore, but a brief rest and some food had left him ready to cope with whatever else the day might have to offer. He loaded both his guns and left one in the pocket and the other in the holster on his good side. His shoulder was still aching but the wound was healing fast. He could get her to look at it. He found a smile playing about his lips at the thought and realized that perhaps he was allowing himself to become attracted to her. This was something he had tried not to do in the past because of the complications involved, but if he really was going to settle here he might as well have some compensation for doing so.

As he rode into the yard of the Greene property he was heartened to see that there was not a single trace of the young woman. It was evident to him that she had learned her lesson well. He hitched up his horse and strode into the yard.

'Anyone around?' he asked.

Annie appeared near the cottonwoods at the other side of the clear area. She was looking at him with a strange expression on her face. She did not say anything but ran towards him as he stood there looking tall, lean and mean in his long black coat. She stopped in front of him, wrapped her arms around him and gave him a warm embrace. He felt her firm young breasts against him and knew that he was aroused. It was almost worth the pain. She felt him wince slightly, let go of him and stepped back.

'Sorry, I forgot about your shoulder.' She still held him by his lower arms as she looked into his face. It was a sight that would have repelled many, but her eyes were filled with a different emotion from that of fear and disgust, both of which the sight of his ruined face had aroused in the past. Then she was leaning forward, standing on her toes, he bent his head towards her and he kissed her on the lips. Her mouth was as soft and warm as he had imagined. She no longer felt like a daughter to him – that was for sure!

'The men arrived – at first I thought it was more trouble from the town, but they told me all about how you had hired them to work for me in getting the place into some kind of order. They were older too, and real nice. I showed them what I wanted done with the fields and the livestock, what there is of it, and they went to work immediately, said they were relying on you to settle with them.'

'If this is what I get for paying for hired help, guess I'll go into town and ask for a couple more. Truth is I expected to be here when they arrived.'

'What just happened has nothing to do with that!' She laughed and punched him on his good arm, which made him press forward, gather her in his arms again and kiss her once more. He pulled back and looked into her eyes. He saw nothing there but happiness and knew at once that he had as good a reason for staying as he ever had. From the way she held on to him, he reckoned she felt the same way.

'Where's Brand?'

'I guess you better know. There's been a murder in town; I expect the guys told you.'

'They didn't, but the sheriff's been here asking if I had seen Brand and I told them I hadn't seen a trace of him. They looked around the place but didn't find a thing. I heard who had been killed.' She lifted her chin and gazed straight into his face.

'I'm not glad that awful man is dead. It's a terrible thing to take a human life, but I'm relieved that I won't be seeing him any more.'

In a few short sentences Thorne told her about the accusation against the employee who had become his friend.

'The sheriff obviously kept it from you in case you tried to give him some kind of warning. Well, he's out of it now. Bradley and his men will be so busy scouring this valley they'll never catch up with him.'

'Do you think he did it?'

'No I don't. He's better off where he's gone to.'

'I'll fix us all something to eat,' said the girl. 'The men brought in some fresh supplies with them. I expect that was something to do with you as well.'

'Could be.'

They all had their meal together as promised, with Pat and Andy promising they would return on the morrow. The miners departed and the two were left alone in the shadows of the early evening. She did not have to say anything because her eyes held a promise he was not going to refuse.

'I have to see to my livestock,' said Thorne, 'now that Brand is gone. It's a pain, but there it is.'

'Why don't we both go over to your place?' asked Annie. 'I only have a few sheep and chickens and they largely look after themselves. The men are doing the rest. Then I can help you out and stay the night.' Her eyes searched his. 'If you don't mind me being there that is.'

'I guess I don't mind the help staying over.' He gave her one of his rare smiles and she punched him on his good arm again. 'I'm just glad you think you can leave here without the place being taken over.'

They began to saddle up, taking their time and enjoying each other's company.

Once more there was the sound of clattering hoofs and the sheriff appeared without his two deputies. He looked

107

weary; they had been searching for the presumed killer of Bug Lannigan, but he had other duties too. He dismounted from his horse and came towards the happy couple holding a folded document that he had taken out of his saddlebag. Thorne was guarded, as usual, waiting for what the lawman had to say. To his credit, Morton Bradley did not look comfortable about what he had to do. In the meantime Annie herself turned her unsuspecting features towards the sheriff, a happy smile playing about her lips. Yes, her family might still be gone but she had at least found someone whom she could love and trust.

'You seen any sign of that heathen?' asked Bradley, addressing Thorne with a faint air of disgust that had never been in his voice before, as if he now actively disliked the gunman.

'Nope,' said Thorne stolidly.

'We're just going back, if we see him we'll let you know,' said the young woman, unaware that the sheriff was looking at her with something like pity.

'I've just come to tell you Annie, you had a common-law claim to this here farm, I can't doubt you, but I'm here to ask you to get off this here land.'

'What?' The young woman looked bewildered.

'Sorry, there's no other way of putting it.' Bradley held out the document towards her. 'As a representative of the law I've been asked to serve this notice on you.'

She opened the document and looked at it with a bewildered look on her face. Just when she thought all was settled there was this to contend with. She studied the words for a few seconds. Thorne had rarely seen such a transformation brought about in a human being.

'I don't understand,' she said.

One minute she was sparkling with zest and interest, the next she was dull, her voice becoming flat, her shoulders stooping as if all the life had been sucked out of her by the contents of the deposition. She looked at her friend in a way that would have seemed impossible just a few minutes ago. It was a look akin to the one that the sheriff was giving him too.

'Can I have a look at that letter?' Dully she handed it over to the former gunman. Thorne scanned the contents of the document in seconds. It was a legal notice announcing that the lands and contents of the Greene spread had been claimed under the thirty days notice that was law around these parts and were to be transferred immediately to the named person. The named person was Jubal Thorne, his signature at the bottom of the form. Thorne handed the letter back to Annie.

'I don't know anything about this,' he said.

'That your name on the deposition?' asked Bradley.

'Yes.'

'That your signature upon the bottom?'

'It's mine all right, but I didn't sign. That's a forgery.'

'Mr Thorne,' Bradley's voice was cold, contemptuous, 'it's bad enough you do somethin' like this to a harmless young woman just tryin' to do right by her family, but on top of that you manage to slur one of our top citizens. On top of *that* you employed a murdering heathen. No one liked Bug, but he was one of our own. You better be real careful about what you say or do.'

'Annie, listen to me, this has nothing to do with me.'

'You'd better go,' she said, her voice hardening in a way that just a few moments ago he would not have thought possible.

'Annie you have to listen to me.'

'I trusted you,' she said.

' 'Fraid you're the one who'll have to go,' said Bradley to the girl. 'Get your horse. I'll get you into town, you can lodge with me and the missus. We'll help you get over this. Leave Mr Thorne to his property.'

Annie slumped her shoulders. All the fight seemed to have gone out of her.

'I'll do it, for now,' she said. She walked past Thorne without a word, fetched her coat and put it on because the evening shades were drawing in and the heat of the day was beginning to fade. She fetched her horse and rode out behind the sheriff without a backward glance, leaving Jubal Thorne all alone in the yard with just his thoughts and the gathering twilight.

CHAPTER THIRTEEN

There had been times in the past when Thorne had been in the middle of a desert miles away from human contact of any kind, yet those were nothing compared to how alone he felt right now. He had nobody and nothing. At that moment he felt like throwing it all away. He had worked hard for nothing and now he was bereft of the one thing that could have given him any happiness, just for doing the right thing.

His shoulder gave a twinge of pain as he got on his horse and headed back to his own home. Except it wasn't home to which he was heading. The homestead was just another place to which he had to go, and he had to attend to his livestock, which he did with a heavy feeling in his heart. Well, it wouldn't be hard to continue looking after the animals, because on the morrow he would just ask Pat or one of the other ex-miners to take over. It was his property to do with what he wanted. He went in and found a bottle of Scotch that he kept for medicinal purposes and made sure that he took his medicine several times.

He was far from drunk, but the alcohol lowered his inhibitions. He practised with his left hand, but still the arm hurt unbearably when he tried drawing a weapon. As for fighting the forgery, his mind told him not to bother.

111

He didn't want to be here, so what was the point? He was leaving, that was all there was to it. He went to bed and after long, drawn-out stretches of time he fell into a deep dreamless sleep.

Annie woke early, could not help herself from doing so. For one thing it was the first time she had slept in a proper bed for days since setting up the hideaway in the woods with the help of – her normally smooth brow furrowed at the thought – the man who had betrayed her.

The sheriff had a surprisingly cosy domestic set up. In a town like this one where everything was central, his house was situated only a short distance from his office. It meant that he was home every night except when he was on duty and had to be up divesting drunks of their guns and throwing them into the cells. His wife was a cheerful woman called Amy who was about five years younger than her husband, and who had given him a little boy and girl, both of whom were less than eight years old.

Given how she felt, Annie was surprised to find that she was able to eat a breakfast of eggs, bacon and beans cooked for her by Amy, who seemed to be an early riser but cheerful with it, something that Annie had never managed. In her old job she had slept mostly until noon, so that might have had something to do with it.

Morton Bradley asked her to walk outside with him once they had all finished eating. Because it was still early in the morning, some of the cold that descended during the night was still in the air and she put on her green woollen coat to go out with him. She had put on her one dress the previous day in expectation of seeing Thorne and had not had time to dress in a more practical manner, having left everything behind at the old spread. She looked very young and a little frail and the sheriff looked at her from time to time as they walked.

'Didn't think that badly of the man,' said Morton as they strode along. 'I reckoned he had some fire in him, but that ain't a bad thing when so many around here are cowed by old Earl.'

'Thorne thinks that you're Earl's man, just like Bug,' said the girl.

'Does he, by heck?' said Morton. 'Well he got the wrong end of that particular stick. When old Bailey, the last sheriff was around you could say that Earl called the shots, but that was ten years ago and more. I was elected by the townsfolk. Before that I was a cattleman, but I wanted to settle down and bein' a sheriff ain't so dangerous if you know what to do at the right time.'

'But why are you walking me out here and speaking to me like this?'

'Sometimes a man needs space to think about a situation. One of my deputies was investigatin' the fact that some sick person was takin' potshots at this Thorne. Sounded like a genuine complaint to me, but now I know how downright annoyin' and slippery he is, can't say as I blame the shootist.'

'I don't understand what that has to do with me.'

'Young lady,' suddenly Morton Bradley stopped in his tracks and stooped in front of her to look in her face. 'Sometimes a man has to do somethin' that's distasteful to him when he's in my line of work. Like having a person feel bad and distressed when she knows the truth.'

'If there's something you need me to do, I'll do it.' She had a firm chin that she lifted in the air as she spoke.

'Well out there – at the fields, my deputy saw some strange markings on the edge of a ploughed field like digging had been done not long before and that was at odds with the ploughing.'

113

'I think I know what you're saying.'

'Then you'll go?'

For an answer she turned and began to walk towards the place where she had stabled her horse the previous night.

It wasn't long before the sheriff joined her along with his two men, Todd and Bob, and they all headed out towards the Thorne spread. The girl did not say much during the journey, but the three men were impressed by her quiet dignity. Bradley had made sure that he brought with him some long-handled spades like the ones used by the undertaker – in fact they had been borrowed from Hardin who was happy to make them available without asking too many questions, knowing that he would learn the answers soon enough.

It wasn't long after this that they were at the field where Todd had made his observation, the very field at which Thorne had experienced the attempted shooting. Annie could see why Bradley had suggested to the landowner that some disgruntled native might have lain in wait to murder the settler. She could see the end of the valley from here and the rough road that led to Dead Man's Ravine where Donald had been discovered.

The men set to work but Annie was not content to stand by; she grabbed a shovel off one of the deputies, Bob, who did not object too much because the heat of the day was coming through, and dug furiously with the other men. The grave was not too deep and Bradley was able to bring proceedings to a halt a short while later. He got Todd to pull back Annie firmly but gently, and finished the last, most revealing part of the dig on his own.

Using his spade delicately in contrast to his raw-boned appearance, he uncovered the pathetic sight of three decaying bodies, all dressed in everyday clothing. All were female as was evidenced by the hair that clung to their skulls, fair hair like Annie's.

Worst of all, two of the skeletal remains were those of young girls, obviously below eight years old.

Bradley suddenly seemed to age ten years. He flung down his shovel and straightened his back slowly. He looked at the young woman who stood there dry-eyed but with her hand to her mouth.

'I'm sorry Annie.'

'Arrest the bastard,' she said, 'and I'm coming with you.'

When they got to the side road that led to Jubal Thorne's dwelling, Bradley gave a signal and Todd rode his grey beside the old mustang that Annie had ridden since arriving there. Todd grabbed her bridle and diverted her from going down the road, making sure that she travelled onwards towards her own homestead.

'Sorry,' called out Bradley. 'This son of a bitch is dangerous and I don't want the possibility of you gettin' harmed.' He waited until the pair had ridden out of sight and only then did he leave with his remaining deputy to confront the man who he now considered to be a vile murderer. Bradley had killed a few men in his time, one or two during the range wars and a few more after becoming sheriff. He had even presided over several hangings. But he had never taken the life of a woman or a child and those he had killed would just as readily have killed him if they had the chance.

The building stood there, a solid piece of work built by Frank Thorne and a testament to hard labour with white-washed walls and solid fencing around. Bradley was not about to go in with guns blazing. Thorne did not know that he was a murder suspect now, along with his heathen sidekick. Of the two, the sheriff would much rather have had it that Thorne had killed Lannigan. At least that way there would have been a lot of sympathy for him and even the possibility that he wouldn't hang. It didn't occur to him that he might extend the same courtesy to Brand, who was the actual suspect in the other case.

'Come out Thorne,' said the sheriff, standing well back from the doorway of the building. There was a stirring from within and the suspect appeared still wearing his signature black coat, an expression of mild surprise on the expressive side of his face.

'I thought we had our little chat yesterday sheriff. How can I help you today? You'll be pleased to know, I've decided to move on.'

'You're not going anywhere,' said Bradley. 'There's a little matter of murder to deal with.'

'So because the half-breed as you call him isn't available you've decided to pin Lannigan's unfortunate demise on me?'

'I never believed you killed that jasper,' said the sheriff, 'but I do believe you killed that woman and her two girls.'

'They're dead?'

'You don't seem to be all that surprised, mister.'

'With the things that've been happening around here, no I'm not, but that doesn't make me a killer.'

'That will be decided in due course.' The gun the sheriff had been holding all the time he was addressing Thorne was raised level. 'Don't try a thing or you're a dead man. Hands up, Thorne. Bob, get his gun.'

Bob came forward, reached into the holster and took the weapon. Both he and the sheriff exhaled a sigh of relief.

'Bob, get his buckboard and attach the horses, cuff his hands, tie his legs and we'll throw him on the back.

Thorne, the bodies were found on your land. You're under arrest for murdering an adult woman and two children. God have mercy on you, because a jury sure won't.'

CHAPTER FOURTEEN

When Annie got back to her own place she found two confused men standing in her yard. In the extremes of yesterday and that traumatic morning she had forgotten all about Pat and Andy. They greeted her with smiles that quickly turned to puzzlement when they saw the deputy.

'Everything all right ma'am?' asked Pat and she saw the world through his eyes. Here was a man who had found a job that would give him some measure of dignity in his life and provide him with some much-needed funds.

'It's all right, boys,' she said, forcing a smile. 'The sheriff has got it into his head that with the shootings going on around here, not to mention what happened to Bug, that I need a bit of protection. Anyway, Todd here is just going, aren't you Todd?' She smiled sweetly at the deputy.

'I guess you're right ma'am,' said Todd, tipping his hat to her. 'Miss Annie, just let me say, when this is all over, if you ever want to meet, socially that is, it would be a real pleasure.' He heeled his mount around and trotted it out of the yard before she could even reply, but she had seen the rapid blush that spread across his young features, and for some reason this pleased her greatly despite the circumstances. She decided to level with her employees.

'I've had terrible news, my sister and their children are dead, killed by a monster in human shape.' The two men were shocked.

'Who done it?' asked Pat, knowing well that not every murderous crime could be pinned on a perpetrator.

'It was Jubal Thorne.' Her words produced only a shocked silence in the two men. 'The sheriff's arresting him right now.'

'Well,' Pat was chewing on a cud of tobacco, which he shifted nervously from one cheek to another as he considered the matter. 'We met Jubal when he hired us, and the other two agreed that Mr Thorne was a gent of the old school.'

'I don't believe it,' said Andy bluntly.

'Their bodies were found in a shallow grave not too far away, on his land.'

'That don't prove a thing,' said Pat. 'You say it was shallow? Then some interloper dug it in a hurry, while if it had been Thorne he would have used one of the canyons outside the valley. It wouldn't have been right of him to do it, but he wouldn't have left a trace.'

'Look, you can both stay on, but let's not talk of this, any more. I have to go into town and fix up a decent, Christian burial for my good sister and two little ones who never did anybody any harm.' She almost broke down at that point, but straightened her back, got on her horse, which was still saddled up, left them a few instructions and rode off to do her duty – alone.

He had been in many desperate circumstances in his life, and that was what sustained Jubal Thorne as he lay there cuffed and tied up on the back of the buckboard. The sheriff and his remaining deputy rode up front, but would have guarded him better if they had known whom they were dealing with. He worked away at the handcuffs under his body, hands jammed behind his back, his slim, almost double-jointed fingers probing away at the structure of the metal. Once he found a weakness he worked away at that too, gradually sliding his slim hand from the cuffs that the sheriff had thought were so secure.

Once his hands were free he would be able to untie his lower limbs with ease. Because they had just wrapped a rope around and tightened it with a hitch-knot, he would struggle his legs out in seconds.

He was attempting to escape at this stage because he knew that once in Earlstown jail, he would find some difficulty in escaping. As the carriage moved along, once or twice, Bob would look round and down at the prisoner, but since the cuffs were behind his back, Jubal still seemed as helpless as a turkey that had been trussed up for market day. Satisfied, Bob would look back at the road again.

Soon Jubal had freed his fingers. He lay there holding the cuffs so that they did not rattle in a loose manner. His bad shoulder was hurting like hell, but he was waiting for the right time, and tried to ignore the pains shooting through that side of his body. The right time came when Bob looked around, saw the prisoner still apparently secure, and looked back at the road again. They were going as fast as they could and the buckboard was rattling up and down as they traversed the uneven road, which meant that with no reins to hold on to, the deputy was in serious danger of being flung out his seat every time they passed over a hump in the road, which, in his opinion, was far too often.

Thorne was about to make his move when he was helped from a completely unexpected source. The sound of a shot rang out, cutting across the line of the horses' progress. These were animals that had been trained in a rough school and were used to noises and sudden appearances of traffic from the opposite direction, but they drew the line at bullets being aimed near them. One gave a frightened snicker and tried to go in one direction while the other came to a complete halt, snorted and pawed at the ground.

The result was entirely predictable. A rider in such circumstances would have jumped off the animal as fast as he could. The two in the driving seat had little choice because the buckboard rolled over, taking them and their passenger with it. Or in the case of Jubal Thorne there was no passenger to fall off the carriage, because as soon as he heard the shot he made his move and threw his protesting body off the tail of the vehicle.

No more shots came from the roadside. Having already been injured in such an attack Jubal was reluctant to proceed with his next move, but felt he had no choice. The horses, feeling the weight behind them, had calmed down because they could not move any further, but the buckboard was now lying slewed over on its side.

Sheriff Bradley and Bob were lying on the road atop one another. They were dazed but unhurt, with Bob cursing at the top of his voice. Confused, they pulled free of the now useless vehicle and stood up. They were faced by a dark figure that looked even more sinister and ghostlike in the dust that still clouded the air around the crashed vehicle.

'Gentlemen, give up your gun belts,' said Jubal. He was holding the Peacemaker that he had kept in his pocket, the one that Bob had foolishly overlooked earlier.

'Don't try to be a hero,' said Jubal as Bradley undid his belt and threw it to the ground. 'I might not kill you, but a bullet wound can sure take a long time to heal, and you won't leave me any choice. Kick over them gun belts.' The two men did as they were asked. Leaving the belts where they lay, Jubal commanded the two men to walk over to a large jumble of rocks at the side of the road. 'Turn around with your hands on the back of your heads,' he said.

'You won't get away with this,' said Bradley. 'Soon the whole town's gonna be looking for you. You're a dead man Thorne.'

'No time to argue,' said Thorne, turning his Peacemaker around and swiftly bringing a crashing blow down on each of their crowns in quick succession. He had done that before too, knew exactly how hard to bring down the blow. Both men flopped down like rag dolls.

Jubal felt an itching between his shoulder blades as he went about the next part of his business, but he had the sense to make a quick survey around the rocks and bushes where the shot had come from. He found nothing.

He fetched the ropes that had bound him lately, tied up the two men, trusting his own knot-tying ability more than theirs, and dropped off their gun belts a few yards away. He freed both the horses from the shafts of the buckboard and jumped on one. He knew this was a busy road and he didn't have much time. Confident the men would be found in due course, Jubal Thorne rode away from the scene.

Annie was riding into town when she came to a fallen buckboard lying on its side. One of the horses was still there, standing patiently at the side of the road. She halted her horse, got off and walked around the wreck. Her view of the other side of the road had been concealed by some long goose-grass, but now she heard the groans of another human being and ran over to have a look, only to find Morton Bradley looking up at her as he sat there,

122

back against a slate-grey rock, his hands bound. His deputy, Bob, was still unconscious.

The sheriff did not have to say anything. She untied him and he looked at her as she freed his companion. The two of them got the man to his feet and he too began to wake as they helped him walk up and down.

'Bob's lighter than me,' said Bradley, 'he can ride on your grey with you, Miss Annie. I'll take the sorrel. We'll get into town and rouse a few helpers.'

'You both need to go and lie down for a while.'

'No time for that, we've got us a criminal to catch. The murdering jasper. As for you, you'd be better off stayin' in town for a while until this blows over.' She did not argue any further but got on her horse along with Bob, who was dusty and sweating and not very pleasant to be around, but somehow his solid frame made her feel safe as they rode back into town to bring the news. The other deputy caught up with them, having decided to make sure she was safe on the way into town.

Jubal was not a man who tortured his mind with thoughts of what had happened or what could be. He only knew that he was grateful for his escape, although he was still puzzled about who had been shooting at the buckboard from the jumble of greenery at the roadside. The question did not fill his mind for long. If he had any sense he would get out of town and ride away across the desert to the nearest place where he could lie low for a while until the whole thing blew over. For a man who seemed so alone he had plenty of friends in the Territory who would help him out when he needed them.

The problem was that the sheriff seemed like a man who was determined that he was going to catch the ex-gunman, whom he now regarded as being a criminal of the worst kind, who would kill a mother and her two young children for personal gain. Jubal found his mouth tightening into a thin, grim line. That at least was one aspect of this sorry mess that he did not blame on the sheriff. Jubal Thorne did not like those who would do such a thing either and would probably go above and beyond the call of duty to bring down such a man. Thorne was innocent, but he had a feeling that if he were to have a personal meeting with the sheriff, Bradley would shoot first and study the facts afterwards.

He was riding Spirit towards his own homestead. This, he realized, was a rookie mistake. He got off his horse and led him into the nearest field where he patted him gently on the muzzle after taking off his reins and saddle.

'Sorry boy, can't let you be part of this. You're too well-known. Stay here and have yourself a good feed of alfalfa.' Spirit whickered and tried to follow his master, but Jubal again commanded him to stay where he was, and his last loyal companion remained in the field while Jubal, walking at a slow pace because he was carrying the equipment he had just taken from the horse, walked to the back of his stables.

He knew that he did not have much time before a party from town showed up, but he was far enough away, and had gained enough time to know that he would be able to make his escape if he moved quickly. He was thirsty, hungry too, but he didn't have enough time to eat. Instead he went to the well, pulled out the bucket and filled up with slightly muddy water. Feeling slightly refreshed he saddled up a brown called Bo, making sure that the cinch straps were well tightened, then went into the farmhouse and fetched his Winchester and a fresh supply of bullets. The Winchester was fitted into a saddle sheath. He had both his Peacemakers because he had recovered one that had been taken from him out of the sheriff's belt, where it had been stuck for safekeeping by that official.

He had with him now a canteen made of goatskin that he had filled to the brim, and a supply of dried, smoked meat, because he knew he would need something to sustain him while he was on the run. He almost laughed out loud at the thought. Jubal Thorne, scourge of outlaws, a bounty hunter extraordinaire, now a hunted man just like those he had tracked down over the years. He knew that he was entirely innocent, but he looked guilty to the world and that, when you thought about it, was all that mattered.

Altogether about an hour had passed since he had tied up the two men. He knew that if they had been freed quite quickly that would mean that he would have to get into hiding, and soon.

He needed time to ruminate over his problems and that would never happen if he were chasing from place to place like a wounded animal. He needed shelter and needed it soon. There was one place he could go, and he turned the head of his animal in that direction as soon as the thought came to him. If he succeeded he would buy time; if not he would get his head blown off.

He headed for Annie's place.

Annie did not waste any time when she was in town. She went to the lawyer's office and asked to speak to him. Spendlow was in proper leering mode as she walked though the door after alerting her presence to the young clerk.

'My dear lady,' he said. 'What an unexpected pleasure.'

'Good afternoon,' she said, instead of smacking him bang in the middle of the face with her fist, which is what she felt like doing. 'I've come here about this bit of paper saying my land belongs to Jubal Thorne.'

'Yes, most unfortunate, looks as if he's claimed every-thing at the head of the valley. It's a local law, you know. Mrs Greene didn't do so, but he did.'

'Maybe she was ignorant of the facts and didn't know she had to put in a claim for the land on which she was actually living.'

'Perhaps so, but the law is the law.'

'Well Thorne is now a wanted criminal, who is strongly suspected of killing my sister and her two children. . . .' Here Annie stopped and sobbed as the full impact of what she was saying rolled over her. Spendlow came over and rubbed her back in an over-sympathetic manner. Her skin crawled at his touch and she pulled away.

'There there, don't take on so,' he said.

'I want to revive the claim in my name,' she said. 'I take it the town won't give the land to a wanted criminal?'

'Certainly, that will be fine, I'll see to the paperwork. There will be a small charge, but you should acquire your sister's land immediately.'

'Good. Thank you. I have to leave now, I hope you understand.'

'Of course, I hope they catch this Thorne guy, he's really been a pain in the side to this town since his arrival.' He led her out of the office and the front door, hand on her back all the time. She wanted to shrug him off like the loathsome creep he was but kept her feelings well concealed because she needed his help.

Her next port of call was the undertaker, Hardin, who stood there rubbing his hands together like white worms as she told him about the discovery of her family. He was immediately in professional mode.

'I will send my men to fetch the bodies,' he said. 'It's not unusual for people to pass away outside their homes in this area, so I am used to fetching – deceased – your sister and her children will be buried within the next forty-eight hours. A sad end, but these things have to be dealt with. I hope they catch that vile murderer. He'll swing for this.'

Satisfied that she had done everything in her power, Annie got back on the grey and began to ride out of town. It was now afternoon and once more the day was hot and clear. She was met by the sheriff, Bradley, who stood in front of her mount.

'Where are you going Miss Annie?'

'Home.'

'Don't you think you'd be better staying in town until all of this blows over?'

'He knows better than to come near me.' A grim smile played about her lips. 'Besides, I have helpers now.'

'Let me send one of my men with you, at least until you get home.'

'No, you need them both for your search.'

'I don't think he's stupid enough to hang around,' said the sheriff. 'He's probably halfway to Colorado by now. OK ma'am, if you insist. We're ridin' out that way soon anyway.'

As Annie rode back to what was now her home, her anger began to not exactly fade, but she began to wonder why the gun she was carrying had been provided by the very man who was accused of murder. Surely he would have wanted to keep her at his mercy if he had been intent on getting the land? She was not some little housewife who listened to the voice of authority and obeyed without question. The reason she was out here in the first place was because she wanted to lead life on her own terms. Jubal Thorne was attractive to her, and that made him dangerous. He too seemed to have a disregard for authority that verged on the reckless.

Then she thought about the way the bodies of her family members had been buried on his land. He had a lot of acres, and once a field was ploughed and sowed with seed, as long as the irrigation ditches were working properly, there was no reason why he should visit that field at the very edge of his land for weeks. The bodies had been buried in a shallow grave not in the field, but off the edge of the area, which meant he would not even see what had happened on his land, if someone else had done the deed.

As she dismounted from her horse and put him into the stables, Annie felt a certainty coming over her that this situation just wasn't right. Not just because of the land claim and the murders, but even through the document that had been presented with the name of Jubal as a claimant. He had been made to look like a greedy, conspiring kind of man, yet he had helped her, seemingly oblivious to his claim.

As she stepped out of the stable she found a hand being clamped over her mouth and the barrel of a gun being pressed against her back. She recognized the musky smell of the man immediately.

'Promise you won't scream,' said a familiar voice, 'don't want to do this, but we need to talk. Just nod your head if you're going to be silent.' She nodded her head and turned as the pressure of the hand was relaxed to find that she was looking into the piercing blue eye of Jubal Thorne.

CHAPTER FIFTEEN

Thorne thought he was fast, but Annie was young and before he could react she too had a gun in her hand. It had been concealed in the folds of her dress and as she pulled away from him the weapon had fallen naturally into her grasp. She pointed the gun at his forehead.

'Killer,' she breathed. 'You're going to die.' She had been coming round to him, but the way he had ambushed her had caused serious doubts in her mind.

'Annie, this doesn't have to happen.' She realized his gun was levelled straight at her chest. It was a Mexican standoff. If she shot him now he had ample time to pull his own trigger, which he would do without any hesitation of he really was a killer like they had said.

'You killed my sister for your own gain, you bastard,' she said, 'her and two little mites who never harmed a soul in their lives.'

'I've never killed a kid in my life,' he told her softly, but with a subtle edge of anger in his voice. 'To me you were inexperienced, soft, I helped you for that reason. I was protecting you.'

They continued to level their weapons while looking at each other. Inside his own head Thorne was trying to predict what would happen if he took the next step. He decided to maximize his chances of survival by backing away from her towards the gloom of the stables where his outline seemed to merge with the dark shadows of the doorway. At the same time he did something he had never done in his life before when there was a live weapon pointing at him.

He lowered his Peacemaker.

'Annie, I just have this to say. I never killed any of those people. I knew your sister and I liked her. The other reason I helped you was because I had let her down. The reason I held you up there was because I thought you were so angry with me that you might commit some rash act without thinking. Think about it, why would I help you so much if I wanted this land?'

'But there was a document with your name on it.'

'Yep, and I figured that one out too. I signed some documents to take over the running of the place when my brother died, and at the funeral parlour, and at the records office. My signature's all over the place. That deposition the sheriff brought saying I made a land claim was a patent fake.'

'Why would they do that in front of you? There was a chance it wouldn't work.'

'That's simple enough to figure out. They didn't reckon I would be here, simple as that.'

'What if I don't believe you? That this is some story just to make me drop the gun so you can kill me?'

'I could have killed you ten minutes ago but I didn't. Remember, I was the one with the drop on you.'

This was such a patent fact that for a moment she had to digest what he had said. Then she lifted the gun more firmly in her hands because it was so heavy that her arms were beginning to tremble.

Annie gave a great shout of rage.

Annie fired.

*

An innocent beech tree beside the barn swayed as the bullet took it somewhere in the middle as it received the token of all her anger and grief. Annie let the weapon drop and threw herself into Thorne's arms. He swayed a little as she came to him because he had been weakened by the events of the last few hours, and his shoulder still hurt like hell, but he was not about to let her go.

They remained like that for several minutes that seemed to pass in seconds, and then he released her and stepped back.

There was a crashing noise from the tree line as one man came in from the fields and the sound of running footsteps across the yard as the other came from the farmhouse.

Pat and Andy appeared, both distinctly out of breath because of their age, but they were both armed and ready to respond to danger. Besides a slight feeling of annoyance at their sudden appearance, for purely selfish reasons, Thorne was pleased that Annie had two protectors who were ready to come to her aid at such short notice. The girl stood in front of Thorne who was nearly invisible in the darkness of the doorway.

'It's all right men; I was the one who fired. It has nothing to do with our new guest. I guess it was all that pent-up rage and annoyance I was feeling at what was done to my sister and her wee ones.'

Thorne stepped out of the doorway. He smiled grimly at the two men who still had their weapons trained on him, fearing that it might be some kind of trick. He knew that they were older and slower, that he could dodge one and drop the other if so needed, but this was one of the times when words would do.

'Just the fellas I need to see. Now who has a bottle of Scotch lain by?'

The next day, instead of going to their new job, the two labourers turned up at their old haunt, the Skull Bucket. The barkeep usually opened the pace an hour before noon, but they had figured on that and turned up just as he was opening the doors. They soon found the man they were looking for when Henry Jones Esquire, former proprietor of *The Town Crier*, came through the door looking more than a little worse for wear, evidently having slept in his clothes the night before as he had done for several weeks.

'Mr Jones, we have a scoop for you,' said Pat. 'We need you to come with us.'

'I'm out of the newspaper game,' growled Jones. He had not eaten much lately and looked as if a gust of wind could have blown him away.

'You're comin' for a little drink with us,' said Andy, 'simple as that. Let's go.' They allowed him one whiskey to fortify his constitution for the trip, then showed him the bottle that would be his reward. Even then Jones wanted to sink into a corner and nurse the headache that was his customary reward for the night before. Pat got him into the passenger seat of a buckboard that he vaguely recognized, but it was not until they were heading out of town that he stirred and came to life. It was overcast for the time of the year and there was a chill in the air that was not usual for this time of day. Jones stirred and showed some of the backbone that had once made him the fearless champion of the townspeople.

'Where the hell are we going?' he asked.

In the meantime Andy stayed behind and it wasn't long

before he found the company of his two old friends. It had only been a few days but already the inn seemed a strange place with its low ceiling and dark smoky air as it filled up with cowpokes and merchants all eager for their midday beer. Bat was the first to swing through the door. For a man who had the lower part of his left leg missing he could move fast enough using his crutch. He was followed by old Tomms who coughed loudly every now and then, pausing to gasp as he tried to breathe in as much air as his ruined lungs, ripped to bits by the mine dust, could take in.

'Boys, it's good to see you again,' said Andy. 'Beer'll be here in a mo.'

'Good ta see ya,' said Tomms as they settled in their usual place. 'Game o' poker? We're down to matches now.'

'No,' said Andy, 'I've been sent here to sound you both out. You know what's been happening with the mines. We all do. Mebbe it's time we made some sort of stand.'

'I can't even stand on both legs,' snapped Bat, who could be a little fierce before his first beer.'

'No use,' said Tomms, 'ain't nobody going to listen to an old man and a cripple.'

'Well mebbe there's a way.' The beers came to them via the barkeep. 'Drink up gents, I have a proposal to make.'

He had paid for the beers – that at least was enough to make them listen to what he had to say, and Pat was a persuasive speaker.

Dickie Spangles was on his way to the office of his employer. He came from the miners' rows at the back of Earlstown, but he was a bright enough lad. At school he had shown an aptitude for reading and writing that had been far superior to that of most of his friends. Dickie had been mocked by his schoolmates for his abilities, but his teacher, Miss Dyer, had seen something in him and had recommended him to Mr Spendlow, the lawyer, who was looking for a clerk to help him with some vague, unspecified paperwork that he had to deal with.

Dickie was going down one of the alleyways that led to the main town when he found his way blocked by a shadowy figure. He felt panic clutch at his throat. After the murder of Bug Lannigan a lot of lurid rumours were going around. He did not want to be the next victim of a throat-slashing, one-eyed maniac. Then the figure stepped closer and was caught by a ray of sunlight slanting between the buildings, and he was cheered to see that it was Miss Annie.

'Dickie,' she said, 'I want you to give me a hand with something. Would that be all right?'

'I have to go to work miss,' he replied carefully.

'Don't worry, I'll send a message that you are sick today.'

'What's this all about miss?'

'Well I know you're good at paperwork and I have some documents I want to ask you about.'

'Couldn't you do it through Mr Spendlow?'

'I could, except I thought this might be the way for an enterprising lad like you to make some money on your own account.'

This was what helped to swing the balance in her favour, for Albert J. Spendlow was currently snowing his clerk under with paperwork. Dickie had been angry about this for a while, because no matter how hard he worked he was paid the same wage.

Besides, Annie was looking particularly beguiling today He was going to spend the day in the company of a pretty woman, getting paid for doing so.

'I'll do it,' he said.

In the meantime Bat and the old-timer were making their way across to the Gold Rush. It was a place neither of them was used to employing as a watering hole for the simple reason that the prices were almost double what they were in the Skull Bucket. On the other hand, the Gold Rush wasn't flooded out during the monsoon season.

The former miners had enough money to buy a few drinks there and they had a mission. As the two elderly men, one on his crutch, swung into the bar no one gave them a second glance. It was nearly empty. People were just too busy working to come in here at this time of day.

Most people were too busy, that was, except for the three men who sat there with drinks at their sides playing poker at one of the round tables close to the door. Old Tomms fetched the drinks for himself and his companion, taking them over to another round table beside the three men. He sat down with his companion, took out a deck of cards and shuffled them while Bat was getting settled.

'Variation on poker with wild cards old-timer?' he asked Bat.

'Who are you calling old, old man?' snarled Bat. He was not acting; it had taken it out of him getting up those five stairs on his crutch.

'Strange thing about that there Jubal Thorne,' said Tomms as he dealt out the cards. The name piqued the interest of the three men at the next table. They froze in the act of playing cards and waited.

'Pat was in earlier, told me that Thorne, he's comin' to town to clear his name,' said Tomms. 'He'll be here any time soon.'

A thin, wiry man got up from the other table and stood beside the two ex-miners.

'You sure about this old-timer?' he asked.

'Not that it's your business, stranger, but that's what I heard. Guess he'll be wantin' to speak to the sheriff and a few others.'

'He won't be speaking to anybody,' said Clarke, pushing away from the table and leaving his cards. 'He's going to wish that he hadn't murdered Bug. Come on boys, let's go and give him a welcome reception he'll never forget.' All three men were armed with their Smith & Wessons, all three had been drinking, but not a huge amount. They knew what they had to do to protect their territory, to get rid of the intruder. They knew they could not be accused of murder. Thorne was a wanted man.

The two men left, watched, as the rest hurried out to take their positions to slaughter Thorne on his arrival. Tomms shuffled the cards and put them face down.

'I better see this,' he said.

Bat glared at the table. 'Guess I'll just stay here and finish these here drinks. I can't shuffle out of the way as fast as you can, you old fool.'

A moment later he was all alone in the saloon. Even the barkeep was gone. He had heard about the fight between Thorne and Lannigan. He wasn't going to miss this one.

Annie let the clerk slip off the back of her big brown mare before dismounting to stand at his side in the small expanse of the yard. He looked about, seeming more than a little bewildered to be here, but she walked in front of him and turned with a smile that was more than a little beguiling. Like most young men of his age he was more than susceptible to the opposite sex and it had already registered with him that Annie was indeed an extremely pretty member of that species. He hurried forward, his youth and inexperience overcoming his intelligence as she led him into the dwelling that she could now live in without fear of eviction. He came up short when he saw a dark figure standing in front of him in the interior of the building. He felt a shiver of fear as if a spirit had appeared.

'You frightened me,' he said to the figure, then gave another start of fear when he recognized Jubal Thorne. He turned and would have run away if it had not been for Annie blocking the only way out.

'It's all right,' said Annie, 'Jubal just wants to ask you a few questions, you'll be paid as promised. No one saw us slipping out of town together, so you won't even be in trouble.'

'That's right,' said Jubal, 'just give a few honest answers and Annie will get you back to town quicker than you can fry an egg.'

'You won't harm me?' asked the frightened boy.

'No, I won't harm you,' said Thorne so mildly that the young man had no choice but to believe him. 'That's better,' added the gunman as the clerk calmed down, but still stood there looking a little scared.

'I just want to know something about Miss Annie's land.'

'I don't know a thing,' said Dickie miserably.

'I know you don't draw up legal documents, that's the job of your boss, but I just need to know, who was the named person on the claim for this land? Right at the beginning I mean, just after the death of Donald.'

'It was Jackson Earl,' said Dickie just as miserably as before.

'When did my signature appear on the claim for this land?' The young man looked straight at Thorne.

'I never saw anything like that at all. The boss does a lot of the paperwork, 'cept lately, he's snowed under. He's—'

'Yet the claim was made and served by the sheriff under

137

your name,' said Annie, suddenly indignant, speaking to Thorne, angry at the act of forgery.

'It's all right Annie,' said Thorne. 'I just have one more question to ask Dickie here, then I'll let him go with his just reward. I saw some rolled-up papers when I was in your employer's office the other day. What kind of papers were they? They weren't legal depositions, of that I'm sure.'

'They were the results of surveys,' said Dickie, 'that's all I know.'

'Land surveys?'

'Yes.'

'And who were these land surveys for, if I may ask?'

'Sir,' Dickie looked miserably at the ground, 'if anyone asks about this in the future it's going to look bad for me.'

'All right, you don't want to answer that one with a name. That would be something to do with Jackson Earl too, I'm guessing.' The young man did not say much but there was a look on his smooth young face and a sudden expression of fear in his eyes that told Thorne all he needed to know.

'All right, get out of here. Tell anyone you want that you saw me.' Annie did not have any trouble getting Dickie to follow her. When she stood aside he practically ran to her brown mare. They got up as before and Annie galloped with him to the edge of town. She hurried back to her own place. She knew that they would not have much time once Dickie got into town and spread his news as he surely would.

Thorne was already waiting in the yard along with her two helpers, a gun holstered at his right side, another in his pocket. This would have been bad enough, but Pat and Andy had appeared with two horses that they had evidently taken from his own stables, all saddled up and ready to go. Thorne had also fetched his own horse, Spirit, from the meadow in which he had been at pasture.

'What in the name of the devil are you doing, Jubal Thorne?' she demanded.

'It's time to fight the system,' he said with a twisted smile. 'That kid told me all I needed to know.'

'To tell the truth, I was kind of disappointed in him, it seemed to me he didn't have much to say.'

'You know when you're trying to solve a puzzle?' asked Thorne. 'Sometimes that one piece is missing and you can't figure out where it should go? Well that little guy just put paid to any doubts I might have had about what's going on in this town. These guys provided the rest.'

'Pat, Andy, what are you up to?'

'We figure if a one-eyed man is going to stand up for what he believes in after all he's gone through, then I guess we can do the same.'

'I told them it wasn't their fight,' said Thorne, 'except they think it is because of what's gonna happen around here.'

'Thorne, if you ride into that town every hand will be turned against you.'

'You really think so? Then it would be useless to ask you to give me a hand, sure could use one.'

'But you were in hiding one moment, now you're taking on the world.'

'That boy confirmed what I had already thought. They thought they would evict you on a technicality not knowing we were friends, but they tried to get me through murder.' His mouth set into a thin, grim line. 'I won't deny I've killed a few men in my time, but mostly they tried to kill me first, and the rest were scum, killers who had taken the lives of innocent people long before I encountered them.'

'Then what can I do for you that's so important?'

He told her.

CHAPTER SIXTEEN

The four riders came into town, three men and a woman, riding four abreast. Thorne was the first to get off his horse and ask the old-timer at the livery to look after it for him. He nodded to Annie, who remained seated on her brown mare. 'You know what you have to do, you'll be fine if you go right now before they spot who's here.'

'This is going to be dangerous for you,' she told him, seeing that facts were facts, her young face crumpling into lines of worry.

'Tell me something I don't know, will you? 'Sides, it ain't my problem that they'll be coming out to get me – it's theirs. Now you get off and do what has to be done.' He was standing beside her horse as she spoke. The girl leaned over and managed to kiss him because he was tall enough to do so without her getting off the horse. Then she straightened up and rode off without looking back. He admired her for doing that, because she knew what terrible danger he was in, yet still trusted enough in what she was doing to leave him with his two friends.

True to his word, Thorne waited a few minutes to give the girl a head start. She knew exactly what she was supposed to do with regard to Jackson Earl, and if things

141

turned out the way he had planned she wouldn't be going there alone.

The inaction nearly killed him, but he forced his companions to wait for at least ten minutes in the shadow of the livery. It was afternoon by then and some of the heat had gone from the air, but the town was not busy because it was a weekday. He used the spare time to instruct his men.

'Get your guns ready boys, but don't shoot unless you have to, and only when someone shoots first. If either of you ended up labelled as killers I couldn't forgive myself. I'm going to be in the lead so I should be taking most of the flak, shelter in doorways when you can, and take your lead from me.' He did not explain that he was hoping to avoid any involvement from them altogether; it was just good to have someone there who could back him up.

He did something that they had not seen before, casting aside his hat and pulling back his coppery hair so that his face was completely exposed, the ruined side distinctive in the bright sun. Then he pulled up the eye patch so it was lost in the fringe of hair at his forehead. This was not Jubal the farmer they were seeing, but the man once known and feared as Blaze, the bounty hunter. It was Blaze who was leading them into battle, the eye in his skeletal socket glaring as he walked.

Taking the lead by quite a few yards as promised, Jubal Thorne rounded the corner into Main Street, boldly walking down the road in the full sunlight. Up ahead he saw the figure of old Tomms, who had been set the task of alerting his would-be attackers. If Annie had known this she would have called it madness, but then so was coming to town.

Tomms immediately vanished from view through the doors of the Gold Rush saloon. He had completed his allotted task, now it was time to see what would transpire.

It wasn't long before the inevitable happened and a gun cracked nearby, a bullet spitting into the ground close to Jubal Thorne. He was passing the bank at the time, and the bullet seemed to be a signal for the beginning of some kind of war. As soon as the first shot came it was followed by a succession of bullets that came from different parts of Main Street, all aimed at the man now seen as an outlaw. This might have had serious repercussions for Jubal Thorne if he had remained in the same spot. However, even before the first shot landed he had swiftly moved across from the road and on to the boardwalk. He did not even stop there, but seemed to melt into the doorway of the bank. This was achieved through the fact that the double doors of that building were painted black. It had often been said of Jubal that he could make himself invisible, and now he was proving to the world that there was some truth in the rumour. He was also helped by the fact that there was an overhang that covered the boardwalk all along that area to protect customers from the heat of the day. This also cast a shadow in the afternoon sun so that anyone aiming at the boardwalk beside the bank was really shooting randomly into a shadowy mass.

Thorne was not wasting his time just standing there and hiding. He was using his brief respite from the gunfire to assess just where the shots had come from.

He knew that the first had come from the side of the undertaker's office across and up the road, the second had come from the alleyway beside the Gold Rush saloon and the third had come from yet further along the street and beside the lawyer's domain. Having finished his survey, knowing they would eventually come and get him, Thorne immediately did what he was best at and ran out into the sunlight brandishing his gun. He would far rather have had a weapon in both hands but his left one was still refusing to work properly, which meant that he could not fire with that side. This did not matter to him because he was not about to let his body be caught in any kind of crossfire. Instead he rolled to the ground and loosed off a shot towards the undertakers as he did so. The door had been partially open to act as a shield for the gunman who had started the whole business. With his acute sensitivity Thorne had even recognized the man; it was Clarke, one of the three remaining vigilantes. The door was not much protection against a bullet from a Peacemaker at that range and a second after the shot rang out there was the noise of splintering wood. The startled man who had thought he was concealed jumped into full view. He was to regret doing so and it was the last regret he would ever have. Thorne fired a second time, and Clarke pitched forward on to his face with a bullet in his heart.

Thorne did not have time to celebrate this minor victory because another figure was firing at him from the safety of the alley beside the Gold Rush. Thorne made a strategic retreat back into the shadows where he seemed to melt away again. But this was only a temporary measure. He knew that if he remained where he was he would be a dead man, and this proved to be a correct forecast because bullets rained upon the area from two directions. A few customers were huddled inside the bank building and there was a serious danger that a stray bullet might hit one or more.

The street had cleared when the fighting broke out. Pedestrians and riders were not about to become involved in a revenge battle that had nothing to do with them.

Thorne decided that he had to take the risk and jumped away from the walkway and zig-zagged across the street, needing that kind of angle for two reasons. Once across the road he was out of the line of fire for one gunman and could draw a bead on the other. His sore shoulder throbbed and he cursed the fact that he could only use one gun at a time.

Luckily there was nothing wrong with his legs and his boots kicked up yellow dust as he moved like a flying shadow across and up the street. This bold move enabled him to see the man who had been shooting along Main Street. It was Jacob Pine, who did not look too pleased to be visible to his enemy. He shot wildly at the moving figure then melted back into the alleyway beside the saloon. From what Brand had told him, Thorne knew that the alley was blocked off by a brick wall. He knew that Pine could not go far, and simply raised his Peacemaker about the height of a man's chest and fired off three quick shots in a row, each of them into the dark shadow of the gap, and each about an inch apart. He knew a thing or two about bullet trajectories and this would mean that he was covering the entire width of the narrow entrance.

He knew the truth of this a few seconds later when there was a loud groan of pain and Pine staggered out of the alley clutching at his chest.

'Murdering . . . bastard . . . you done for me,' he gasped, his gun dropping from his nerveless fingers.

'You're dead mister,' said a cold voice, and Thorne looked round to see that Binns was bearing down on him along the boardwalk, gun in hand, about to squeeze the trigger. He had obviously thought that while Thorne was dealing with his friend it would give him the chance he needed. The would-be killer had forgotten that he was dealing with an experienced fighter or he wouldn't have shouted out his message. Not that Thorne was unaware of what was happening with regard to the appearance of the last thug. What a triumph it would have been for Binns to say that he had killed the mighty Jubal Thorne. He would have lived off the kudos the news would have brought for the rest of his life.

Thorne ducked down and threw his body to one side as the bullet from the Smith & Wesson roared harmlessly over the spot where his head had been. He pulled the trigger of his Peacemaker and nothing happened. He had run out of bullets.

Thorne did not hesitate; he straightened up, still facing Binns and ran towards the man, doing so on the roadway, his feet raising more puffs of the thin yellow soil, and as he ran he reached into his coat pocket.

'Got you,' shouted Binns as he saw the weapon being cast aside, and let off a couple more shots, both of which missed because he was not taking proper aim in the excitement of seeing his prey without a weapon. Like his friends he was not a gunman, but an ex-miner who was not well-versed in the use of firearms. Most of the time he had relied on the presence of his compatriots to avoid any actual fighting. This was all to the good for Thorne, who decided, quite reasonably, that if a man tried to blow his head off three times, that man was a viable target. Thorne pulled out his spare Peacemaker from his coat pocket and fired at a range of just a few yards. The force of the bullet was such that Binns was actually lifted off his feet, flew backwards on the boardwalk and hit the lapped wall of the building with a distinctive thud. He pitched forward and fell to the boardwalk on his face, with a hole a man could have put his fist inside in his back where the bullet had emerged.

It was at this point that the sheriff came thundering back with his two men, riding up Main Street on their horses, having heard the shots from some distance away, while they were still out hunting for the man who was standing there with a still-smoking gun in his one good hand. Thorne paid the horses no mind for the moment, but went over to the roadway and picked up his cast-aside Peacemaker and holstered it. Only then did he look up at the figure that was already dismounting and striding purposefully towards him.

'How do Sheriff Bradley?' he asked.

CHAPTER SEVENTEEN

Annie had never been surer of the rightness of anything in her life. Long before the battle began on Main Street she knocked at the door of the Earl House, the name of the mansion at which she stood. Instead of some liveried servant it was Earl himself who answered the door. He was wearing a dark suit and had the look of a man who was in the middle of doing something important. He was also rather crumpled and unshaven looking, with a distinct air of weariness about him. His handsome, firm features had somewhat dissolved under pressure. Jackson Earl was looking old.

'Young lady! Do I know you?' he asked.

'Annie Bateman is the name,' she said. 'You might have known my sister, Agnes Greene.'

'Ah, sad business that. But it's not a reason to bother me at the moment.'

'Get inside.' She levelled the gun at his chest.

'If I shout out one of my men will be here in seconds, and you will be a dead woman Annie. They won't let your obvious good looks deter them from protecting me.'

'Get in there, don't try anything. We don't have much

time.' Earl moved backwards as requested and she saw immediately that she had been right to call his bluff. The beautifully appointed hall of the mansion, decorated in silvery wallpaper with golden borders, was distinctly unkempt in appearance. Any incidental furniture was gone and boxes lay everywhere, some still open with clothes, paintings and other items visible, although nothing like the amount of possessions a rich man might have been expected to own. 'Thinking of leaving town?' she asked.

'A man can leave town when he wants,' said Jackson Earl with a subtle edge of menace to his voice. It was obvious that he was thinking about the fact that she was a young, slim woman, while he was six inches taller, built like one of the bears he loved to hunt, and she was alone.

Annie saw the look on his face and gave him a smile that he did not like.

'Henry, come in, it's all right.'

Henry Jones, once the proprietor of the local newspaper that had been destroyed by fire, taking his livelihood with it, walked in and stood beside the girl. He did not seem to have a gun, only a notebook and pen.

'Walk around,' said the girl, 'take a look at all the finery, what's left of it, it shouldn't take you long.' Jones took off at once with an intent look on his face that he must have worn once, before the fire in his offices had taken away his will. He was back within minutes with a paragraph or so written on the paper. It was lucky that he had taken so little time because it was obvious that Jackson was bracing to attack the girl, who had just stood and stared at him with her liquid eyes while the newspaperman was looking around.

All three jumped when the sound of gunshots could be heard from Main Street.

'Time for us to go,' said Annie. 'I sure hope you've got a couple of horses and a carriage left in those fancy stables out back.'

'Why?'

'Because you're going for a ride.'

'Sorry about this, Thorne, I thought you were an honourable man, but you can't be allowed to go on. Arrest him boys, we're going to have a hanging.' The two young deputies grabbed Thorne, one on either side; he winced in pain but did not resist, even letting them take his Peacemakers, all the while staring at the sheriff with that strange half-skeletal face that he usually kept so well concealed. A large amount of the populace was present now that the battle was over. Men, women, children, everyone had emerged from where they had been concealed during the heat of slaughter. The sheriff halted with his men under the yardarm outside the jail, went inside and came out with a length of rope with a hangman's noose at one end. Morton Bradley liked to be prepared. As the rope was pressed into service, flung through the gap in the yardarm, noose brought down to the height of a man, Bradley looked around the crowd with faint defiance. Thorne was at his side, held by the deputies on the porch just behind the noose.

'This hanging ain't for the crime of shooting those three dogs. They attacked first, that's been on the cards for a while. A man ain't guilty of defence. This man's going the way he should because of what he done to that woman and her two little 'uns. He's a real killer this one. We're well rid of him.' He stopped and pushed Thorne in the back, the gunman stumbled forward and looked at the crowd without any emotion whatsoever as the noose was put around his neck. The thing was, there was nothing for

Thorne to stand on that could be kicked away, then he saw with the stark clarity of one who was going to die that there was an iron hook screwed halfway into the timber pillar that held up the porch roof. He was going to be jerked off his feet and held up there, rope wound on to the hook, with an ever-tightening noose around his neck until he was strangled to death.

'Say your prayers,' said Bradley, 'because you're goin' to hell where you belong.'

At that moment the door of the undertaker's office burst open and Hardin was led out by two men, each holding a gun to his head. A carriage rumbled down the hill and the crowd parted like a tide as the dark steeds bore relentlessly forward. Even before the horses came to a snorting halt in front of the jail three figures alighted from the carriage, one a slim woman, another the rumpled form of the town's founding father, Jackson Earl. He stumbled forward but the girl held a gun to the back of his neck. The third figure came out of the carriage, also armed, and seemed to disappear into the crowd.

'Stop!' commanded the girl.

'Miss Annie, this ain't ya business,' said Bradley. Then his eyes widened as the crowd parted again and the two ex-miners came forward, a gun on either side at the head of Pate Hardin. There was a shout, and then a big man in a white linen suit was pressed forward and at his back holding a pistol was the thin ghost of a newspaperman, his eyes rimmed with red and an expression that said there was another death pending that had nothing to do with Thorne.

'What the hell?' Bradley reached for his gun, and his two deputies did the same. Thorne twisted like a bolt of lightning out of the noose and snatched his own Peacemaker from the belt of Todd, where it had been thrust for the moment. He smashed the weapon down on either man's head in quick succession and they flopped to the ground. Bradley turned to shoot him dead and found a gun in his back. It was Pat, who had left Hardin in the charge of his companion.

'Listen to what the folks have to say,' he said reasonably. Morton had no choice but to turn to the semi-circle of captured men held there by weaponry.

'Tell him,' said Henry Jones to Spendlow, 'tell him right now.' There was no doubting the savagery in his voice. This was a man who had already lost everything and when you have lost everything you have lived for, sometimes your life doesn't mean all that much to you.

'It's – he's forcing me to say this,' said Spendlow.

'Don't say a word,' said Earl with low menace. 'Or you're finished for good.'

Annie punched him on the back of the head. 'Shuttup. You'll have your say.'

'I did the contracts,' said Spendlow, 'the new contracts for the railways. They're coming to town, all the surveys have been done, the work will commence soon. It's a good thing, it's going to save this town.'

'Then tell us why Jackson Earl is leaving,' said Jones savagely.

Incensed, Earl began to jump towards his right, where the lawyer was being held. This time Annie, emulating Thorne, smashed him on the side of the head and stuck her gun hard into his back.

'Try again, you're dead.'

'Earl is leaving because his business here is done,' said Spendlow. 'A man has a right to go where he wants.'

'Not when he's lied for years.' Suddenly Thorne moved forward, looking at the men in front and the crowd behind, his glinting eyes catching their attention. 'I think

Henry Jones has something to say about that.'

'Jackson Earl is bankrupt,' said Jones. 'He brought this snake in to manage his affairs because he needs money.'

'The mines are played out,' said Thorne, 'he's known they were going that way for years but he said nothing. What did you see in that mansion?'

'I saw an empty shell,' said Jones, 'his wife, his daughters, the fancy furnishings, they're all gone.'

'You see when you have a wife and two daughters with a taste for the high life they don't last for long in a mining town,' said Thorne with a twisted smile. 'Earl was quite happy bossing it over his little kingdom, but then he felt the pressure on top of him from his family and his massive gambling debts. He kept opening new seams in the hope of finding silver, but he finally had to face the truth. That's when he hatched his plan with Spendlow and Hardin – as founder as well as mayor he could do anything he wanted without question.'

'I had nothing to do with it,' shouted Hardin.

'Shut your blame mouth,' said Earl with a look of menace that quelled the man for that moment.

'With the help of this snake,' Thorne pointed at Spendlow, 'he found out how to claim common land, and then he set out with the help of Hardin to file a claim for every piece of land he could get. Didn't you?'

'You're a liar and a murderer,' snarled Earl. 'People, can't you see what he's doing?'

'Shuttup,' said Annie savagely. 'I won't tell you again.' She thrust the cold barrel of the gun into his back.

'You see, Hardin, being the undertaker, would tell him when a farm at the head of the valley became vacant and Earl would claim the land. Only two families stood in the way at the end. The Greenes and the Thornes. They weren't too much trouble, because Frank Thorne, who

owned the biggest farm, died of a heart attack so the claim
was filed immediately. That was messed up when I came
along. Donald Greene was out of town on business when
he mysteriously fell down a ravine. His wife and two
daughters were abducted by a thug called Lannigan,
working with Pate Hardin. Look at who's got the tools for
quick burial. Pate also decided to get rid of the last major
pest – the man who had replaced Frank and who had
blocked the last claim. I can prove it too – look in
Spendlow's papers and you'll see what he gets for every
deal he pulls off to get the land for Earl.'

'That's a lie,' yelled Hardin.

'Is it? Just like the fact that when the railway finally
comes to town you're going to get a cut every year until
the day they put you in one of your own boxes. That's in
the papers drawn up by Spendlow too. You made sure of
that. Sheriff, make sure that the lawyer's office is
sequestered for examination on those lines.'

'I will,' said Morton Bradley grimly.

Pater Hardin had a thin line of a mouth but he was suddenly urged to speak as he tried to tear away from Andy. 'I
should have shot you in the head. Would have too if it
hadn't been for your cursed luck.'

'I knew it was you,' said Thorne calmly. 'You hid and
tried to kill me twice, it's just your style, to work away in the
background. What's the matter, couldn't hit me in a field?
Can't track a moving target? The only one I don't understand is when you tried to help me when I was being run
into town by the sheriff.'

Hardin looked confused at this.

'What are you talking about? I didn't have anything to
do with that.'

The strange thing was, Thorne believed him. Not that
he had time to think about this because Earl suddenly

twisted around because the girl had been distracted by grief for her sister, when Thorne was talking the undertaker. Earl managed to pull away from her. Worse was to follow; he was a big bull of a man and he took the weapon out of her hand by simply crushing her slim fingers around the butt of the gun until she had to let go out of sheer pain. Then, when he had the weapon in his possession he pulled the girl in front of his body as a shield from all weapons that were suddenly pointed at him. Calmly he held the gun to her head.

'I'll get out of here, with this woman and no one will get harmed. I'll let her go when I'm away from this dump.'

'Don't listen to him,' said Thorne calmly. 'He'll kill her just like he killed Lannigan.' This time it was the sheriff's turn to look startled. He had been about to reason with Earl, now he turned his attention to Thorne.

'What?'

'He didn't want Lannigan to reveal the extent of his involvement in what was going on – so he followed Bug into town one night, waited until he came out of the saloon to make his way home and slit his throat. Then he raised the alarm, got you and your men out searching when he was the guilty one.' As he spoke Thorne moved forward calmly, his eyes glittering as he waited for a chance to use his Peacemaker.

'That's a damned lie,' shouted Earl, still backing away with his arm around the girl's throat.

'Is it? Then how do you explain the fact that Brand never had a drop of blood on him when we met at the homestead, while you were drenched in it?'

'He told me it was because he was trying to help Bug,' said Bradley, shaking his head at how blind he had been regarding what Earl had done.

'You knew Brand had threatened to cut Lannigan's

155

throat and you traded on the fact that the sheriff would take your side and hardly question you about what had happened,' said Thorne. 'Now let go of the girl and there's a chance that you'll get a fair trial.'

The crowd, who had heard the accusations and saw what was happening to Annie, surged forward and Earl could no longer access the carriage. Instead he dragged her towards the alleyway on the far side of the Gold Rush. Once he was in the back streets he could get away, not least because this was his town, he knew every nook and cranny and could get help to escape.

But this was not his idea at all; he knew that a man on foot could be tracked down quite easily. He threw the girl to one side with an abruptness that startled everyone, quickly unhitched one of the horses and threw himself on to the startled sorrel. It bucked and almost threw him off, but did not succeed in dislodging the fraudster.

He might have managed to get away from the scene of his disgrace to some kind of safe haven, because he was now on the far side of the crowd and anyone who fired at him would risk hitting an innocent bystander. He was not wearing spurs, but he was an experienced rider, not least in the races that were held from time to time in the Territory. He dug in his heels and the animal gave a snort of pain and annoyance, shooting forward at a speed that would soon take him out of town.

At that second something flew through the air that glinted silver in the afternoon sun. The object flew with a speed and accuracy that had to be seen to be believed and embedded itself in Earl's right shoulder. He gave a groan, instinctively tried to pluck the weapon out, fell off the animal, rolled over on the ground and lay still. The girl ran over to him and managed to turn him over, although others were already running to help.

'He's still alive,' she said, looking up at the sheriff, who was standing over her. 'It's a muscle wound, that's all.'

'Good,' said Morton Bradley, 'because he'll have a good long time to think over his actions when he's in jail along with the other two. Although he'll swing if they can prove he had a hand in murdering your sister.' He turned to Thorne, who had arrived at his side a second later. 'Come on, help me get him inside a cell with the other two, the town doc'll give me a hand to deal with his wound. If he and that slimy undertaker had anything to do with murdering children they'll *both* swing.'

Thorne helped the sheriff jail the three men, until the investigation could be completed, and did this along with the ex-miners and the newspaperman, all of who were willing to appear as witnesses to what was going on.

Thorne faced Bradley on the porch of the sheriff's office. The two deputies had both recovered by then but Bradley restrained them from attacking Thorne. The gunman apologized handsomely and promised them a reward of a couple of hundred dollars each for their trouble.

'I'm mighty sorry, but I had to see this through,' he said, and such was his aura of certainty that they believed him and stood back beside their sheriff.

Morton Bradley looked at him with eyes that were no longer blind to the man in front of him.

'When you escaped, that clinched it for me, 'specially when I saw you killin' those three attack-dogs hired by Earl. Seemed to me right there and then it was a case for action. When a miscreant is rampaging there's enough cause for a summary hanging.'

'It was a risk I had to take.'

'Given who Earl is, ya'll have to testify even though you wouldn't have had that luxury.'

'I will – backed up by Annie and my ex-miner friends, not to mention those who knew about the deals Spendlow and Hardin had made to line their own pockets.'

'Just don't leave for a while.' There was a thin smile on Morton Bradley's lips. He too was alive to the irony of the situation.

Thorne stepped back into the light of day. He had restored his hair, hat, and eyepatch and looked more like the man Annie had come to know. There was still a crowd outside the jail, the numbers swelling when the word got out that the town's founder was going to betray them all and make a massive fortune out of the railroads, while the mines died. There was some unrest, but Thorne stood beside the sheriff, two men with natural authority.

'Go back to your homes,' said Thorne. 'Justice will be done, and when the railways come – as they will – the money'll come into this town, not into the pockets of Jackson Earl.' The crowd began to disperse now that the fun was over.

'You'll have to stick around,' said the sheriff, 'but as far as I'm concerned you're free to go. I always knew that Earl was a strange, twisted man.' He departed to search the lawyer's office.

The girl was in his arms and he kissed her as thoroughly as he did everything else. He let her go and walked down to the alley beside the saloon.

'You can come out now.'

Brand emerged hesitantly, blinking in the sun, hat pulled low over his face.

'You didn't go away,' said Thorne in a resigned voice.

'No, I stay and track you, lucky for you.'

'It was you that fired that shot when they were bringing me into town, the one that got me out of the buckboard. Why didn't you show yourself to me?'

158

'Thought you might be angry with me. Tell me to go. More useful keeping track of you.'

'I was just going to unseat him with my own weapon, Brand.'

'Would have killed him, needed him alive.'

'What can I say? He's right.' Thorne turned and grinned at the girl. 'Let's go home for some eats. I'm bushed.'

'Me too,' she said. The three of them fell into step as they made their way towards the livery.